BAD BOY DONE WRONG

KYLIE GILMORE

Cover design by Sweet 'N Spicy Designs

Published by: Extra Fancy Books

ISBN-13: 978-1-942238-32-4

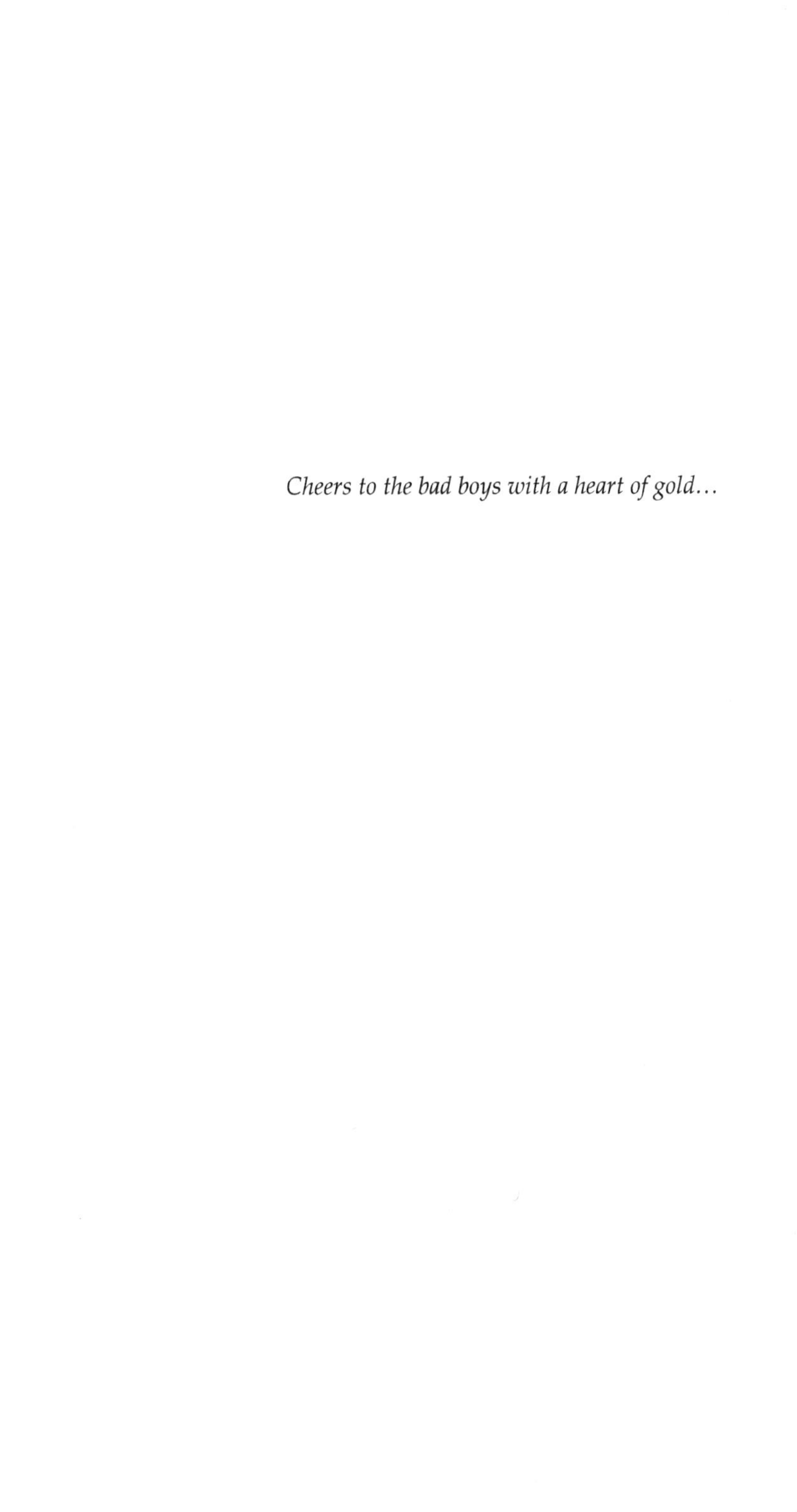

Cheers to the bad boys with a heart of gold…

1
——————

<u>WANTED</u>
One alpha bad boy straight out of romanceland.

Must haves:
Passion <<Most important!
Sexual confidence
Intensity
Deep panty-melting voice
Hard muscular body
Never does relationships

Optional but highly desirable:
Facial hair especially a beard
Gruff and growly
Checkered past
Rule breaker
Tattoos
Motorcycle

. . .

Carrie taped her list to the bathroom mirror, hoping when the magical moment arrived and she finally found the alpha bad boy of her fantasies, she'd have the courage to make her move.

2

———

The Morning After Carrie Makes Her Move…

Carrie Young woke with a satisfied smile, fully prepared for her first ever walk of shame. She propped up on her elbows, suddenly alarmed. Something was very wrong. She was naked in the bed of a strange man's apartment with the delicious scent of bacon wafting through the air. What the fudge!

She jackknifed upright. Was that pancakes too?

Weird. Did bad boys cook breakfast the morning after a wild night of debauchery?

She rolled out of bed and searched for her clothes. She found her purple dress hanging from a lamp where he'd tossed it and the matching bra wadded on the floor nearby. Panties were nowhere to be found. Whatever. She was pretty sure going commando would be exactly what someone who just had a fling with a bad boy would do. She grabbed her purse where she'd dropped it by the bedroom door and slipped on her slutty black heels. But before she could enjoy her walk of shame, she really needed to brush her teeth. She never neglected personal hygiene.

She headed to the adjoining bathroom, pulled a small bag of toiletries from her purse, and inspected herself in the mirror. Yes, she definitely looked ravished. The layers of her blond hair were askew, landing just past her jaw at odd angles. She had beard burn on one side of her neck and her blue eyes were brighter than usual, or maybe that was her new contacts.

She finished up in the bathroom and followed the scent of bacon to the kitchen, where Zach, a tall lean man in his thirties, stood barefoot in front of the stove, expertly flipping pancakes in a white short-sleeve undershirt and dark green tartan plaid boxers. She flashed to a brief *Outlander* fantasy because *tartan plaid*, and his thick dark brown hair was on the longish side, curling at the nape of his neck. He had the kind of sinewy strong body that could easily lift a woman, as he'd fully demonstrated when he (unknowingly) performed item number six on her secret naughty list, euphemistically named Carrie's Wish List.

A girl had to dream. Especially after dedicating six prime years—nineteen to twenty-five—to Edward, her super-controlling, repressed, toxic ex. Why had she stayed with him so long? Maybe because she'd been young and naive, maybe because he'd started off with the most romantic of courtships, or maybe she just didn't know any better, having nothing to compare him to. That time was past. It had been more than a year since Edward, and now she was spreading her legs, er, wings. She'd been looking for the alpha-bad-boy experience because there was just so much she'd missed out on in the bedroom.

Carrie was taking back her womanly mojo.

Her stomach growled. She'd strut out of here right after breakfast. It would be rude to leave when Zach had gone to the trouble of making all this delicious food.

"Hi," she said.

He whirled, a slow smile dawning. He had a full beard and she nearly squirmed remembering the unusual sensation of it brushing against the sensitive skin of her neck and breasts and belly. "Hi, Carrie," he said in a deep honey voice that made her knees weak. If she were wearing panties, they totally would've melted. "Hope you like pancakes."

"I do, thanks."

"Coffee's ready." He gestured to the coffee maker, which had just beeped. "Help yourself." He turned back to the stove.

"You're quite the host." She set her purse under the square wooden kitchen table. Then she tried out the naughty-girl thing on her way to coffee. "Zach, right?"

He turned, his light brown eyes narrowing. "Do you not remember calling out my name multiple times last night? You said you only had two glasses of wine."

She blushed furiously, felt extremely naughty and bit back a smile as she poured herself a cup of coffee in the white mug sitting on the counter. "It's starting to come back to me."

Suddenly he was at her side, taking the coffee from her hand, setting it on the counter, and then cradling her jaw with one warm hand. He tipped her head up and gazed down at her for a long smoldering moment. Her lips parted, her heart thudding in her ears, her body humming in anticipation. He was so much bigger, tall with wide shoulders, she felt petite, even though she was an average five feet five.

He dipped his head, his lips brushing over hers in a whisper of a kiss. "Maybe you need a reminder."

"I do," she breathed, aching for more. Zach had been everything she hoped last night—sensual, insatiable, open to anything. Now he was going to let breakfast burn while he took *wicked* advantage of her and hopefully performed item number one on her wish list.

He bit her lower lip and then sucked it. "After I feed you." His voice was gruff and growly, scraping across her insides. He gazed deep into her eyes, still cradling her jaw, and she couldn't breathe for a moment. Finally, he released his hold on her and swaggered back to the stove.

She wobbled and leaned against the counter, her skin hot, her lower lip still tingling.

He glanced over at her, a small knowing smile playing over his lips.

She looked away, blushing, but then reminded herself she was no longer that blushing good girl, she was a woman who made no apologies about, well, anything. She retrieved her coffee mug from the counter and settled with it at the kitchen table, carefully tucking her dress under her. There was only a half wall separating the kitchen from the living room, which was mostly empty. Just a black sofa with a dark red fleece blanket thrown over the back, TV mounted on the wall, a desk with a laptop, and a bunch of boxes lined up on one side. They were on the first floor of an apartment complex, end unit, she remembered that from last night. Definite bachelor pad. Neat, even. That didn't mean he wasn't the alpha bad boy of her fantasies. He'd already ticked so many of the boxes—deep panty-melting voice, beard, hard muscular body, and most importantly, passion. Plus sexual confidence that made him deliciously dominating and *intense*. Woo! Was he ever intense! Okay, yes, the lack of tattoos was a little disappointing, but all things considered, he'd been perfect for her —sexy alpha with just a hint of bad. She'd sort of pounced on him at the bar last night once she knew he was a friend of her cop friend, Ethan, who'd confirmed Zach was bad to the bone but not in a criminal way. She wasn't crazy, after all, just sexually deprived.

A few minutes later, Zach served her a plate with three crispy pieces of bacon and two pancakes drizzled in syrup.

"Thank you," she said, cutting into the pancake and popping a piece in her mouth. Omigod. It was amazing. He'd even warmed the syrup. She chalked up his gourmet cooking to his extremely sensual nature. Food like this was definitely a sensual experience. He was still her fantasy bad boy. "Are these blueberry?"

"Yeah. They're in season. You like?"

She quickly cut another large piece. "I love them!" It was the first weekend of August and this area of Connecticut was bursting with fresh produce.

"Good," he said gruffly. A shiver ran down her spine. Gruff and growly did it for her for some reason. He filled a plate for himself, sat across from her, and dug in.

She'd nearly finished eating when it occurred to her she forgot to make conversation. The food was just so good and the silence hadn't felt awkward at all. She lifted her eyes to his. He gave her a small smile and kept eating. He was the quiet sort with a steady reserved demeanor, almost like he preferred to sit back and observe. Like a shrink would. Was he psychoanalyzing her? What did he do for a living? All she knew through the grapevine was that he was back home after being in "no man's land" for years. She quickly decided he couldn't possibly be a shrink because Zach's asking in his deep gruff panty-melting voice, "How does that make you feel?" would surely lead to more orgasms than confidence sharing. At least with women. She stifled a laugh.

Ooh! Maybe he was in a motorcycle club and cruised the back roads of outlaw country somewhere out west. Or maybe he led mountain expeditions in remote parts of the world and that was why he had the beard. To keep his face from freezing off. Or maybe he lived in the rugged Highlands, hiking through rocky terrain with only his beard and a kilt to keep him warm. She liked that he could be any fantasy. She was pretty sure this hookup qualified as a one-night stand, so he could be anything she wanted him to be. Unless…

She studied him for a moment, debating if she should share her wish list with him. She hadn't shared it with a guy before, at least not on purpose, but she'd dearly love to experience the other six things on it. Her list had seven items whittled down from the original thirteen, after her friend Ally had pointed out there wasn't much difference between some of the items. For example, "sixty-nine" had a blow job unnecessarily added to what she really wanted—a man to go down on her. She'd done the blow job thing; the other was new. No need to be redundant when she was living on the edge.

Zach leaned back in his chair, folded his hands behind his head, and studied her through his naturally hooded bedroom eyes. So hot. She hoped she looked ravished and stunning, not like her usual bleary morning self. She took another bite of pancake and realized she was full. She eyed the remaining piece of bacon. She really shouldn't overindulge, but it had been so long since she'd had bacon. She wasn't much of a cook.

"Go ahead and eat it," he said. "It'll just go to waste if you don't."

"You can have it."

"I'm good." He watched her, his eyes dancing with amusement.

"Something funny?"

He set his palms flat on the table. "I'm just surprised the woman who took exactly what she wanted last night is hesitating now over a piece of bacon."

Her cheeks heated. He hadn't leaned in, but he suddenly felt close, all up in her space, challenging her. And, dammit, this was the new empowered Carrie. New sexy dress, new contacts, new unapologetically sexy attitude. *This* Carrie took what she wanted, whether that was an alpha bad boy or a frigging extra piece of bacon.

She snatched the bacon and took a bite. Effing delicious.

He leaned back in his chair, seeming satisfied to watch her eat. Feeling self-conscious, she studied the living room behind him with stacks of boxes lined up against one wall.

"You just move in?" she asked.

"Yeah."

He didn't offer any more information.

Still, she had to know something about the man she hoped would continue to rock her world. That might've been presumptuous. On the other hand, she wasn't sure how long it would take her to find another alpha bad boy that ticked so many of her boxes. He'd been downright spectacular last night, bringing her favorite sex fantasy to life—alpha wallbanger. She had to at least feel him out. Maybe he'd be willing to help her out a little longer. "Where'd you move from?"

"Colorado by way of Indonesia."

Wow! It was both out west and exotic. This was definitely a man worthy of her wish list. Nerves ran through her as she debated pulling out her phone and showing him the list in her notes app or maintaining the cool façade of a woman who did the casual fling thing regularly. But if she didn't show him the list, she'd have to tell him what she wanted and she wasn't so sure she could do that. Okay, what was the worst thing that could happen? He'd laugh at her. Best thing? He'd perform every single thing on that list and make her dream come true.

Show him!

No, it's too soon.

He already did number six.

But he doesn't know he did it!

She rubbed her temple. It was one thing to tell your best girl friends about your pathetic love life, a whole different thing to tell a bad boy you just met that because of your pathetic love life, you now had some pretty intense and specific needs.

He took a sip of coffee, completely calm in the face of her turmoil.

This had all been much easier last night with two glasses of wine in her. "Thank you for breakfast," she blurted, falling back on good manners in the face of potential awkwardness.

"Yup." He took another sip of coffee and watched her over the rim.

She stood abruptly, cleared her dishes, and set them in the sink. She ran the water so the syrup wouldn't stick and be difficult to clean later. Then she turned and let out a yelp because he was *right there*. Directly behind her, holding his own dishes.

"Calm down," he said, setting his dishes in the sink. "What're you so jumpy about?"

"Nothing," she squeaked. She took one step around him when he snagged her by the waist.

"Hold on now," he said, turning her to face him. He held her by the hips and pulled her close enough to feel his heat. She was suddenly keenly aware he was only wearing a V-neck undershirt and boxers, which meant it would be so easy to get her hands on his hard body. Her fingers itched with the urge to touch and she was through denying herself. She slid her fingers under the front of his shirt over the ridges of his abs to his warm chest. He smelled like bacon and she suddenly desperately wanted to lick him all over.

"Carrie?"

His deep voice vibrated under her hands and she wanted to rub her cheek over his chest, then press her ear to it and soak that sexy voice in.

He tilted her chin up. "Not that I'm not loving your hands all over me, but I'm trying to figure out why you seem so…unsettled."

She told herself to stop touching him, but her hands wouldn't listen. They slid up over his wide shoulders and then back down his chest over his sexy abs to the waistband of his boxers.

His hands stopped hers, holding them at the edge of his boxers. "We good here?"

This was it. The moment she'd been waiting for in the entire year it had taken her to get up the nerve to approach a bad boy. She'd be a fool to pass this opportunity up. "Can I be honest with you?"

"Yeah."

"You have to swear not to laugh. Not until I leave."

He gazed at her steadily and squeezed her hands. "I won't laugh."

She couldn't maintain eye contact. She stared at his exposed chest at the V of his shirt, tanned skin a few shades darker than hers with some dark hair. He released her hands only to snag her hips, taking her with him as he shifted to lean against the counter. He wrapped his arms around her waist, looking completely relaxed. She was the furthest thing from relaxed, pressed against that hard male body. Her nipples tightened into peaks and she was sure he could feel her heart thudding against her rib cage. She took a deep breath, placed her hands on his warm chest, and risked a look up at him. He watched her with his sexy hooded eyes, and those sensual lips seemed to be calling to her to stroke and taste and suck. A flutter low in her belly and the throbbing between her legs spurred her on. She could so do this.

She opened her mouth, but nothing came out.

He remained quiet. Geez, make it harder for her.

"Ask me anything you want." She needed an opening. A

question that would somehow lead to her explaining and explaining until she finally spit it out.

He gazed into her eyes, his expression intense, his voice gruff and growly. "Tell me why the woman that came for me multiple times last night and wasn't quiet about it either—" he paused, a sexy smirk crossing his features "—is jumpy as hell now."

She flushed and muttered to herself, "Such a bad-boy thing to say."

His lips twitched. "What can a bad boy do for you, Carrie?"

"Okay, I have a list. Okay?"

"Okay."

She got braver. "Seven things to make up for six years of repression. Seven years if you count the year it took me to finally get a taste of the forbidden."

He cocked his head. "Which part of last night was forbidden?"

She patted his chest and then rubbed it. "Good girl-bad boy." It was in all her favorite romance novels. Not as forbidden as, say, teacher-student, but still *far* out of her comfort zone.

He released her. "Let's see your list."

She turned and stared at her purse under the kitchen table, willed herself to go over there and get her phone, but she couldn't seem to move.

"Carrie." His big hand cupped her jaw and turned her back to him. "Nothing on that list will shock me."

He brushed her cheek with his thumb before dropping his hand. She relaxed a little. He'd probably seen it all, done it all. This wouldn't be a big deal to him. She searched his features, checking in with him one last time to be sure he was taking her seriously and not about to laugh in her face.

His voice dropped, gruff and low. "Give me the list *now*."

The hair on the back of her neck stood on end. His eyes were direct and hot on hers. He said nothing more, yet she knew he fully intended to take her list seriously.

With shaking legs, she crossed to where she'd left her

purse, pulled out her phone, tapped in the code, and pulled up the list in her notes app. She glanced at the naughty list she had memorized, felt a belated blush over sharing it, but before she could change her mind, he snatched the phone from her hands.

"Hey!" she exclaimed.

He didn't respond. Instead his brows drew down as he read for what felt like forever. Finally he lifted his head. "What the fu—"

"Forget it!" She yanked the phone from his hands and stuffed it in her purse. "I wasn't here." She bolted out of the kitchen, through the living room, and out the front door.

"Carrie, wait!"

She glanced over her shoulder. Omigod, he was chasing her! In his boxers! He was nuts!

Her fight or flight kicked in and she flew, her legs pumping hard down the sidewalk and then suddenly she was airborne, tossed up and over one large shoulder. The primal hold told her everything she needed to know as he carried her back inside—

She was in trouble.

3

———

The Night Before…

"Finally got sprung from the ivory tower!" His honorary brother Ethan Case greeted him cheerfully the moment Zach stepped into Garner's Sports Bar & Grill for his welcome-home party. Zach hadn't been home in two years. First because he worked in Colorado and spent holidays with his ex and, when that ended, he threw himself into his work and traveled to Indonesia for his research. He'd hoped to make it home last Christmas for Jake's wedding (another honorary brother), but he'd been in Indonesia and contracted dengue fever right before the trip home.

He smiled and took in the face of the brother he'd missed the most. Ethan had the same dirty blond hair with some spikes in front, and sharp blue eyes with a few more lines etched into his face. They were the same age, thirty-four, and grew up in the same foster home, looking out for each other, each in their own way. Ethan made sure Zach didn't get his ass kicked; Zach made sure Ethan passed all of his classes.

"Eth," he managed over the lump in his throat.

"Professor." Ethan gave him a quick one-armed hug around the neck. "Come on, let's get you a drink."

He made his way to the bar through the crowd, mostly the guys he'd grown up with, the Campbell brothers and the ragtag collection of guys like him with troubled childhoods that had all found each other through the Police Athletic League. Joe Campbell, his honorary dad, had been their coach, staunch advocate, and friend. Mad Campbell, his "little sister," was also here with a large group of women friends he'd never seen before. He'd been out of the loop too long. Last time he'd been home, Mad only had guy friends.

Ethan tapped the bar. "Let's get this man a beer."

The bartender and manager of the place, Josh Campbell, grinned and served Zach a beer on tap before saying quietly, "Good to have you back home."

The quiet sincerity in Josh's voice hit Zach like a thump to the chest. He meant it with deep affection. Growing up all close in age, he'd been tight with Josh, his twin Jake, Ethan, and Marcus. Why hadn't he made time to come home to the only family he'd ever known? Why had he let his ex's family take precedence? Or his work?

Because you're a lone wolf.

His ex, Dr. Muriel Hapsburg, a respected professor in the psychology department at the University of Colorado, where they both worked, had pegged him with the label a week after they broke up. Their fallout had been one of those put-up-or-shut-up moments. She'd given him an ultimatum after a year of dating to either marry or break up. His gut said no to marriage. He'd explained it wasn't her. He couldn't picture spending the rest of his life with anyone. She'd returned to his apartment the following week with a box of his things and a small speech that now felt prophetic.

"I'm not angry," she'd said. "I've had some time to process and I understand. Because of your childhood wounds, chosen vocation, and particular interest in observing distant communities, it's clear to me you're a lone wolf. My parents agree. Just do the next woman a favor and don't lead them on with anything long-term. You'll only ruin it."

He'd given it some thought, weighing in the fact that her

parents were also respected psychologists and he'd spent a lot of time with them, and realized Muriel was right. His whole life made sense in this lone-wolf framework. There was no use denying who he was at heart. But even a lone wolf sometimes returned to their pack. So here he was, back in Connecticut.

He reached across the bar and clasped Josh's hand warmly. "I won't wait so long next time." His voice came out hoarse. It wasn't like him to be so emotional. He prided himself on his ability to detach and observe. Something he'd learned as a kid and had served him well in his work as an anthropologist. When you're a nine-year-old repeat runaway, life can do that for you. Yup, lone-wolf behavior went way back. But something about being home again got to him.

Josh gave Zach's beard a tug. "Look at you with a beard. That a tribal thing?"

He rubbed his beard. "It's easier in the field not to worry about shaving."

Josh stared at him and slowly shook his head. "You wear it well."

"Thanks." And then he was surrounded by his honorary brothers boisterously greeting him, pounding him on the back, joking around with him, all of them hyped up with the energy of the gang getting back together. The only one missing was Joe, their honorary dad, who was babysitting his two-year-old granddaughter, Viv, tonight. Zach would be meeting him for dinner tomorrow. He hadn't met Viv yet, though he knew what she looked like. He kept current with everyone, filing the facts away in his head. He texted, emailed, and occasionally Skyped.

Zach sipped his beer, the chatter of the party swirling around him. He was home on a year-long sabbatical to work on his book—the culmination of four years of fieldwork on the forest-dwelling communities on the islands off Indonesia. He'd figured his family would keep him from turning into a complete hermit. He probably wouldn't spend the whole year here, though. He was expecting his application for a two-year senior research fellowship at the Asia Research Institute in Singapore to come through soon. It was a competitive position, but he was a frequent visitor to the institute and the staff knew him and his work. He could continue writing his book there, closer to professionals in a variety of disciplines that could bring broader perspective to his work. So he'd spend a handful of months here, two years there starting early January, maybe back to Colorado, maybe he'd stay in Singapore. Or somewhere else. Couldn't tie a lone wolf down.

He took a pull on his beer. The important thing was that he was intellectually challenged. Speaking of, he mentally reviewed possible angles he could take to shape his book into a nonfiction narrative that would get more eyes on it than just academia. He'd love for the general public to take an interest in his work, which was particularly focused on Indonesia, but also the entire Southeast Asia region.

"Hi!" a feminine voice said loud enough to quiet his rambling thoughts.

He looked down at a gorgeous petite blonde with big blue eyes, a cute button nose, and a beaming smile. Her fair skin was smooth, flawless, glowing with good health, and her purple dress showed off tremendously sexy curves—a perfect hourglass shape. All the classic signs that indicated attractiveness in a woman who could produce viable offspring. Not that he was looking to reproduce, but biology worked for a reason. In keeping with his primitive instincts, the blood rushed through his veins, reminding him it had been way too long. Not since last summer, damn, a year now, when things had gone to hell with his ex.

He pushed that sour memory from his mind. Then he squared his shoulders for the prominent chest thrust and gazed directly into her bright blue eyes. His educational background gave him an advantage with women once he understood—no matter the culture or era—courtship was a dance choreographed by biology. He dropped his voice to the deep tone that signaled domination, a key indicator of a worthy protector and provider for the young he had no intention of producing. "Hello."

"You are *the* man," she said in the most adorable pickup line ever. "I've been looking for you."

He studied her for a moment, taking in her sexy self, before giving her a slow smile as he leaned closer. "Yeah? Where've you been looking?"

She lifted both hands and spread her fingers wide. "Everywhere."

Entertained, he kept asking questions. "Where's everywhere?"

She tossed her jaw-length hair, which bounced around a bit. "Singles mixers, the hospital, here at the bar."

"Hospital?"

"I'm a pediatric nurse. And I know what you're thinking, but a doctor was *not* what I needed." She wrinkled her cute button nose. "Neither was the nurse or lab tech, though they were certainly male and moderately sexy."

He had no idea what to say to that.

She did and spoke right up, the words tumbling out in a rush. "I know this sounds forward, but I've been looking for quite some time and you, *wow*, seriously *wow*, so let me get right to the point—I'd like to do a number of things with you of the naked variety, if you're agreeable."

"I am," he answered immediately. He was no dummy. He snagged her elbow and guided her to a quiet corner of the room. That was when he noticed the sexy black heels. A surge of raw lust gripped him with startling intensity. Some of the guys watched him go, giving him knowing looks that he ignored. "What's your name?" he asked once they had a little privacy.

"Carrie. And you're Zach. My friends told me who you were, so welcome home!" She sang this last part. "Even though we've just met."

"Thanks. How much have you had to drink?"

"Two glasses of wine. My friends won't let me have more because they say I can't hold my liquor." She frowned, looking very put out about that.

He grinned because she just kept getting more adorable.

Also, her hand was now on his chest and she was close enough her sweet vanilla scent was urging him to taste.

She went on. "I have a roommate, Ally. We could go to our place and play loud music to cover what I'm sure will be crazy loud whoopie—"

"Whoopie?" *Did people say that anymore?*

"But I don't want to make her feel bad. She's been down about her dry spell."

"Would you like to go to my place?"

She threw her arms around his neck. "I thought you'd never ask."

His hands went to her waist. "You smell like vanilla."

"It's my body wash." She went up on tiptoe and closed her eyes. "Kiss me, *bad boy*," she purred.

"Sure you're not drunk?" He had to check because normally women did *not* call him bad boy.

She responded by kissing him passionately, and long dormant parts of him responded in kind. He got her back to his new apartment one town over in record time, party forgotten. Once inside his bedroom, she went for it, hands and mouth hungry, kissing, biting, climbing his body. He lost control.

Hot. Rough. Hard.

Pounding, pounding, pounding.

No holding back. Couldn't hold back.

Sweet cries of ecstasy ringing in his ears. Long guttural groans ripped from his throat.

Hours and hours. He couldn't get enough. Neither could she.

By the time she curled up against his side and fell asleep, he was exhausted. In a good way. He closed his eyes, hoping sleep wasn't far off, but he always slept better alone. It was one of those lone-wolf things that used to piss off his ex. Hell, if there was one thing being an anthropologist taught him, he was far better at observing relationships than participating in one. He'd accepted it and now planned his life accordingly.

Carrie mumbled something in her sleep and rolled away

from him, taking the blanket with her. He tugged the blanket, but somehow she got it wrapped under her too. He gave up, dressed quickly in undershirt and boxers, and headed to the living room sofa to sleep with the throw blanket.

He fell asleep with the sweet taste of vanilla on his tongue.

4

———

The Morning After Continued…

Carrie's morning-after glow ignited to sharp need as Zach carried her like a sexy caveman back to his apartment. She landed with a soft plop on his living room sofa. He sat next to her and her breath caught at the massive erection tenting his boxers. She met his eyes, his expression awfully serious considering he was just as turned on as she was. Was her list really that disturbing?

"No one's ever carried me like that," she informed him.

He blinked and continued staring wordlessly, seeming to be waiting for her to say something more.

"I admit it turned me on," she added.

He flashed a smile. "Good to know. Your list is very curious."

She smoothed out her purple dress and crossed her legs like the lady she'd been raised to be. "Is it?" she asked demurely.

"Did you do some research?" he asked, sounding oddly academic about it. "Was it based on the *Kama Sutra*?"

She laughed. "No, even better. Romance novels."

"I'm not familiar with that context."

"Most men aren't. Though it would definitely help with male-female relations. Alpha-bad-boy sex is the best." She got a heat flash just thinking about it.

His large hand settled high on her upper thigh, heating her through the thin fabric of her dress. "Like last night?"

She nodded and uncrossed her legs.

His hand slid to the inside of her thigh, where it stayed frustratingly close but not touching where she desperately wanted him. "Can I see the list again?"

She hesitated, feeling a little squirmy about sharing the list after his WTF reaction. Part of her wished she'd never mentioned it. Maybe she could just act it out with some instructive hand signals.

His hand left her leg and cupped her shoulder instead. "Carrie."

She sighed. "Can you just pretend you never saw it?"

He gave her shoulder a squeeze. "I'm dying to see it again."

She lifted her chin, trying to appear above a shoulder squeeze even as she warmed at the spot. "Why?"

"I'm trying to figure out what everything means."

This was understandable. In fact, she was a little worried she'd been so subtle with her euphemisms that no one would *ever* understand her list. The first list she'd written had been much more explicit. There'd been an incident. She'd meant to text it to her friend Lauren, who'd insisted she take a look at it before Carrie shared it with a guy, and accidentally sent it to her eighty-year-old neighbor Larry. They were next to each other in her contacts. (She was his in-case-of-emergency person.)

Now Larry wouldn't stop smiling at her.

This embarrassing reason for her euphemisms was not something she was prepared to share with Zach despite his fine alpha qualities. She gave him a once-over from thick dark hair to the sexy beard to lean muscular body and, yup, still hard. So very male. Then he startled her with an extremely insightful observation.

"I gave you number six, I'm pretty sure. A wallbanger."

Her eyes widened, impressed he'd read between the lines of her euphemisms. Translating "I'd like to meet Harvey" to "I desperately want a wallbanger" took a smart man. Harvey Wallbanger was one of those dirty-sounding cocktails ready-made for a euphemism.

"I thought this was a onetime thing," she said, hoping he'd say it wasn't. He'd been amazing last night, but she knew bad boys didn't do long-term. If it was more than a onetime thing, *maybe* she'd show him the list again.

He brushed her hair back over her ear. "You'll probably see me around sometimes. We know a lot of the same people. And didn't you say you live not far from here?"

"Yes."

"Then we can be friends and friends share stuff. Wouldn't you like the guy point of view on it?"

He was making a lot of sense. Oh, heck, what could it hurt?

"You're very clever," she said, pulling her phone out again and punching in the code. "Of course I would love the guy point of view. If I'm being unrealistic, or if any of these items are a complete turn-off, it would definitely be best to know before I embarrass myself."

She held the phone so she could read along with him, figuring she'd jump in with explanations where needed. "You see—"

"Wait. Let me read."

She stared at the list and tried not to squirm.

Carrie's Wish List

1. Dessert comes first.
2. Top floor is extra fancy.
3. Sunday drive is sometimes bumpy.
4. Squeaky clean is best.
5. Animals are primal.
6. I'd like to meet Harvey.
7. Call me Bond. Jane Bond.

She glanced over at Zach, his face an expression of fierce concentration. It reminded her of his intense focus last night and she felt her entire body soften.

Finally, he nodded once and she tucked her phone back in her purse. Then she waited, trying to look cool and composed even if she couldn't quite meet his eyes. She steeled herself. This was the new sexually empowered Carrie. Of course she could handle talking about her deepest desires with the sexy man she'd known for fourteen whole hours. She risked a look at him.

He stroked his beard thoughtfully, but remained quiet, studying her.

She broke under the pressure of all that thoughtfulness. "Well?"

He met her eyes with a bemused expression. "That is the sweetest most confusing naughty list I've ever seen."

"Have you read others?"

"No." He stroked her arm, apparently trying to soothe her, but his touch was anything but soothing.

"Maybe it would be less confusing in the right context." *And with two glasses of wine in her.*

"You mean in bed?"

"Mmm-hmm." *Don't feel him up.*

His hand trailed lower, encircling her wrist, his thumb brushing across the sensitive underside. "What does top floor mean?"

"Ah, yes, top floor," she said in a breathy voice, unable to focus because he kept stroking her wrist, which had suddenly become an erogenous zone she had no idea existed.

His voice dropped to a low rumble by her ear, giving her a hot shiver. "Give me a hint. Top floor?"

She stared straight ahead before whispering, "Like I'm on top." At his silence, she took a deep breath and met his eyes.

His brows scrunched together. "Am I the floor? No, wait. Better question, you've never been on top?"

"My ex, Edward, was very traditional. Man on top except for my time of the month when he wanted me to service him in another way."

His fingers tightened on her wrist. "Which way?"

She lifted one shoulder up and down. "Hand or mouth."

He dropped her wrist. "Who got to pick?"

"I did, but I knew he liked mouth better so..." She shrugged.

"And you were with this guy how long?"

"Six years."

"And before him?"

"Just him. My one and only."

"Carrie." He dragged out her name. So much wrapped in one word—concern, desire, protection.

"What?" she asked softly.

"You're practically an innocent. I can't in good conscience let you run around showing random guys this list."

She scowled. "You don't get a say in this! It's my life and I'm done playing it safe." She grabbed her purse and glared at him. "And don't you dare chase me in your sexy tartan boxers or try that primal caveman move because it won't work this time. You've pissed me off and I don't get pissed off easily. I'm usually very sweet and even-tempered."

She stood and headed to the door, a little surprised he wasn't following her. He'd seemed so determined before. She reached the door, hand on the knob, and something made her look over her shoulder. He sat there, studying her like everything she did was fascinating. No one ever looked at her like she was interesting at all. She usually blended into the background. "Well, goodbye."

"I'm not looking for a relationship."

She turned to face him fully. "I didn't ask you for one. Geez, that's the last thing I want after my toxic pseudo-marriage." Honestly, she felt nauseous just thinking about being trapped in another relationship. What if she lost herself again?

At his continued silent staring, she added, "Why do you think I picked you up in a bar, bad boy? Hint: it wasn't for conversation."

He let out something alarmingly close to a feral growl. She sucked in air, simultaneously wary and turned on.

His gaze remained direct, pinning her in place. "I never stick in one place long," he practically growled. "I'll be going overseas the first chance I get."

She wasn't sure why he was still talking to her, but politeness had her responding in kind. "Okay. Not that I expected any different from a bad boy. In fact, that was exactly why I was looking for one. Plus the hot alpha sex. So, um, yeah. Thanks for last night." She lifted a hand in a small wave. "I'll see you around, probably. I live a few blocks away in the condo complex. I'm not sure if you're a jogger—"

"Two weeks." He stood and stalked toward her. "I'll do your entire list in two weeks. You'll get it out of your system and stay safe."

She lifted her chin. "I told you I don't want to play it safe."

He reached her, slid her purse off her shoulder, wrapped an arm around her waist, and with a quick tug she was flush against him, his erection pressing into her belly. Dark desire simmered in his eyes, wreaking havoc on her determination to put some distance between them. He dipped his head and kissed her roughly. She moaned and went up on tiptoe, wrapping her arms around his neck while he took and took and she eagerly gave.

He lifted his head, staring at her with so much heat she immediately wanted to strip naked. "Are we in agreement?" he asked in a soft dangerous tone.

She suddenly felt like she was making a deal with the devil. "You play dirty."

His lips twitched. "I'm glad you think so."

She loosened her hold around his neck and felt up his sexy chest again. "You think two weeks is long enough to do the whole list?" She and her ex only had sex once a week. She really hoped Zach would be available more frequently than that.

He cupped her jaw, his thumb stroking lightly across her cheek. "Definitely."

She squeed and threw her arms around his middle in a tight hug. Then she pulled back, beaming and bouncing on the balls of her feet. This was so ideal. He'd help her out and then cut her loose for her next adventure. He hauled her against him and the perfection of it all hit her between the legs with his next devouring kiss. My Lord, he was an amazing kisser.

When he finally let her up for air, she said, "You got a deal, bad boy."

He gave her a wolfish smile that made heat pool between her legs along with a pleasant throbbing. How could she resist?

She grabbed his ass. "But I reserve the right to skip or repeat certain things depending on how I feel."

"Sure. We don't have to go in order." His voice went gruff and growly. "Bad boys break the rules all the time."

Her breath caught and her stomach dipped at the thrill of it all. He'd just checked another box on her fantasy alpha-bad-boy list—rule breaker. She kissed his neck and then licked it before shifting to rub her cheek against his beard. Next thing she knew, he was kissing her and guiding her backward until the backs of her knees hit the sofa. He pushed her down and dropped to his knees in front of her, his hands already sliding her dress up to her hips, where he found nothing but skin.

Their gazes locked, both of them breathing harder.

His voice was commanding and deliciously dirty. "Spread your legs, naughty girl. I'm about to eat dessert first."

She spread her legs and gave a soft cry, suddenly thankful she'd found herself a smart bad boy.

Carrie practically floated back to the condo complex, which was only three blocks from Zach's apartment. How conve-nient. Zach, man, he got the job done. *Wring me out, limp noodle, and thank you, sir!* She felt euphoric and giddy and tap-dance happy. Immediately following that first mind-blowing orgasm, she'd texted Zach the list. She'd been about to explain each item, but he'd said he liked the challenge of trying to figure it out. Then he tossed her over his shoulder, carried her to his bedroom, and put her on top. Already three things on the list completed!

This two-week fling could not have been more ideal. They'd talked openly and honestly in negotiating the terms. Everything spelled out nice and clear. Plus he'd probably be traveling to wherever he traveled (they'd talked very little once they'd given in to passion) and she was firmly rooted here in Connecticut. In three weeks, as part of the Carrie empowerment plan, she would be going to grad school at the University of Connecticut for her master's in nursing to become a certified pediatric nurse practitioner. She'd been awarded a two-year teaching assistantship that would pay her tuition. As a nurse practitioner, she'd earn a higher salary and have responsibilities similar to a physician. Edward had discouraged her from graduate school, saying it was a waste of money when they already had his ample salary as a brain surgeon. Not that they were married. They'd lived together and he hadn't proposed until four days after she'd dumped his sorry ass for cheating on her and, worse, lying about it. Lying was a hot-button issue for her and she had zero tolerance for it in any form.

Edward had made her feel like an oversexed needy woman for years (when she was perfectly normal!) while he'd been hooking up with random women he met through a kinky sex app. When she'd confronted him with her suspicions, he made her feel like she was crazy. Turned it all around like *she* was the one with the problem. He lied about it right up until she slapped a folder full of evidence in his hands. His excuse? He was keeping her pure as the future mother of his children. Twisted bastard.

That betrayal had cut deep. She'd known him her whole life, their families were close friends, and had looked up to him. He was seven years older, handsome and sophisticated to her young eyes. In retrospect, she'd invested way too much energy trying to keep him happy, walking on eggshells when she did something that displeased him and he'd freeze her out for days on end. Her only rebellion had been attending singles book club meetings with the Happy Endings Book

Club before she was actually single. Not that she ever did anything with any of the men she met as a result, mostly the older brothers of fellow book club member Mad Campbell. But now she was so glad she'd taken that step because the women she'd met there had become the closest friends she'd ever had. Like her roommate, Ally Bloom. It had taken a lot for Carrie to regroup in the aftermath of what felt like a divorce and really think about who she was and what she wanted out of life. Just seeing her friends living their own awesome lives had inspired her.

Out of the ashes of her failed relationship, her true passions emerged. Voila! Empowered Carrie. Sexually satisfied Carrie.

She smiled to herself and opened the door of the two-bedroom condo she rented with Ally, who was just about to leave, already in her swimsuit and terrycloth cover-up, beach bag over her shoulder. They both had memberships at Grand Lake in Clover Park, where they had plans to meet some of their friends. It was a lazy Sunday-on-the-beach day, show up when you could.

"How was it?" Ally asked eagerly, her brows shooting up under blond bangs. They looked similar, sometimes people thought they were sisters, close in height, both of them with blond hair and blue eyes, but Ally had an easily excitable, bubbly personality whereas Carrie was normally very down to earth. Her fling with Zach being more the exception than the rule.

Carrie grinned. "Awesome."

"Yay!" Ally dropped her beach stuff, rushed forward and hugged her. "I'm so happy for you!" Ally knew how much it meant to Carrie to take this step after her ex.

Carrie gave her a squeeze and pulled away. "Thanks. Let me get ready and we'll drive over to the lake together."

"Okay, let me just text..." Ally's thumbs flew in rapid texting probably to their friend Hailey. "Okay." She looked up, her blue eyes bright and eager. "Tell me *everything*."

Carrie laughed and headed for the bedroom.

Ally followed her and sat on Carrie's bed. "Come on! I

have to live vicariously. You know how long it's been for me. Augh!" She spread her arms and flopped backward on the bed.

Carrie pulled her modest one-piece blue swimsuit from the drawer. "He's going to do my whole list."

Ally shot up to a sitting position. "You showed him your list?" she exclaimed. Ally was the one that had helped her with the euphemisms. They'd cracked up, coming up with them over a bottle of wine.

"Yup!"

"And he's actually following it? Isn't the point of a bad boy that there are no rules?"

She laughed. "He'll probably go out of order. Can't expect that much rule following, right?" Her heart kicked into a rapid cha-cha at what Zach might do next. Her limbs felt light and she would've done a happy twirl, but she didn't want to rub her good fortune in Ally's face. Her friend was hung up on a guy from college.

"I knew he couldn't be that bad if he's close with a cop," Ally said. The cop, Ethan, had been pretty psyched at the party to have Zach home again.

"He's not a criminal," Carrie replied. "He's more of a badass."

"What's he do for work anyway?"

Huh. She hadn't thought to ask Zach about himself once she started thinking about her wish list. She'd already told him item number one—dessert comes first—would definitely be on the repeat list.

He'd just given her one of his slow sexy smiles. "I know."

The way she'd grabbed his head and screamed might've been a tip-off. She flushed with heat at the memory.

Ally moaned. "You're thinking about him, aren't you? And the fantastic sex. Ugh. I'm so jealous. Maybe I need a list."

Carrie shook her head. "You don't lack experience like I did. You just need to meet someone."

Ally sighed. "I already met him and lost him."

"Oh, Ally, I hope it works out for you at the reunion." Ally wanted to get back together with her college boyfriend of four years at the reunion next month.

"Me too. We're both single and we've been texting back and forth a lot." She crossed the fingers of both hands, kicked off her flip-flops, and then lifted her feet to show her toes were crossed too.

Carrie put her swimsuit over her shoulder and crossed her fingers in solidarity. "I'm going to take a quick shower," she said and slipped into the bathroom.

"I'll go pack your cooler," Ally said.

"Thanks!" Her friend knew her fave snacks for the beach.

She stared at the alpha-bad-boy list taped to her bathroom mirror and beamed. Mission accomplished. She carefully peeled it off and tucked it inside the small vanity drawer. No need for the reminder now that she'd found him. She quickly showered and changed into her swimsuit, slathered sunscreen on her fair skin, and grabbed a beach towel from the linen closet. After she packed all her usual beach stuff in a large tote, they drove over in Carrie's Toyota, Ollie, which hadn't let her down in ten years of reliable driving. Ally kept pressing her for details on her night with Zach, but for some reason Carrie didn't want to share. There was something about Zach, maybe it was his quiet cool reserve, but it just didn't feel right to talk about him like that. She was sure he wasn't the type to kiss and tell. She finally reported to Ally only the fact that they'd covered three items on her list and it was everything she'd hoped. This seemed to satisfy Ally, who sighed dreamily and told another Dean story. Carrie had never met Dean, but she hoped he was every bit as great as Ally made him out to be.

They found their friends lounging in a group on beach chairs and towels—Hailey, the matchmaking leader of the Happy Endings Book Club, along with Missy, Sabrina, and Lexi. The rest of their tight-knit group was either working or busy with their guys.

Carrie hadn't even taken her seat in her beach lounger when Ally shared, "Carrie found the man for her sex list."

"Shh!" Carrie exclaimed, quickly looking around to make

sure they weren't sitting too close to other people, especially families. Coast was clear. They weren't that close to the water, where most people preferred to hang out.

The women erupted with questions, which Carrie ignored, instead settling into her beach lounger and reaching into her cooler for a drink.

"Carrie!" Sabrina exclaimed, leaning toward her and then shoving her dirty blond hair out of her face. Her volume caught everyone's attention because Sabrina was normally on the quiet side. "You can't just drop a bomb like that with no follow-up." She lowered her voice. "Sex list?"

Carrie offered her unopened drink to Sabrina as a distraction. "Yoo-hoo?"

"Carrie!" the women exclaimed in near unison.

"Stop trying to change the subject," Sabrina said gently.

Carrie focused on twisting off the cap and taking a long drink, not about to share her wish list again. Now that Zach had it, no one else had to know. Finally, the weight of everyone's stares prompted her to say, "Ally said it, not me."

"It was Zach," Ally shared.

"They know who it was," Carrie said, pressing the cold drink to her forehead. They'd all been at Zach's welcome-home party last night, but the guys had monopolized him, so none of her friends knew that much about him. Like her, they only knew Zach was close to the Campbells and hadn't been home in years on account of being in "no man's land." Their friend Mad Campbell was working today or she'd probably have filled them in. Carrie quickly decided the less she knew about Zach, the better. She didn't want to get too attached.

"How was the beard?" Sabrina asked.

"I don't kiss and tell," Carrie said, biting back a smile.

The women eyed her. Their romance book club had started as a singles book club (now some of the members were engaged or married) and they always shared the details of their love lives. She knew she wasn't doing her part, but hell. She was done with doing what was expected of her. She wasn't looking for love. As far as she could tell, love was a quiet domestic arrangement like her elderly parents, or suffocating like her and her controlling ex. Either way, it promised a lifetime of boredom and responsibilities. She wanted *passion*. And Zach was willing to give it to her.

Hailey propped up on her elbows, a vision in pink—teeny pink bikini, pink-framed sunglasses, pink lipstick, and matching polish on her fingers and toes. She was a former beauty queen with long strawberry blond hair, pale blue eyes, and flawless skin with the heart of a die-hard romantic. For other people, anyway, not herself. She was Clover Park's one and only wedding planner, a self-professed love junkie and happy ending facilitator. "I completely understand your discretion, Carrie. You're a classy lady. Speaking of classy ladies, would anyone like to go on a date with Ethan? I'm trying to show the rumor that he's a sex addict wasn't true and that he's a perfectly fine candidate for ladies like us."

The women tittered. Poor Ethan. The rumor of his sex addiction was a whole other crazy story. Suffice it to say, he was *not* a sex addict, but the rumor had stuck, as often happened in small towns. Hailey was determined to right that wrong. She was keen on everyone having a happy ending.

Carrie pulled a bag of potato chips from her cooler and offered it to Hailey. "Why don't you go out with him?"

Hailey waved the chips away. "No time. Too busy building my business."

"But you have time for us," Carrie said, passing the bag to Sabrina.

Hailey sighed and pulled her long hair up, fanning the back of her neck. "Men are work. You ladies keep me sane." She dropped her hair and looked around the group. "Anyone for Ethan? You don't have to be alone with him. I'll get him to Garner's on Thursday after book club. Just smile and flirt so everyone knows he's cool."

"Can't," Ally said. "I'm getting back together with Dean next month."

"I'm with Zach for now," Carrie said.

"For now?" the women echoed in near harmony.

"Once through her sex list," Ally explained. "Not in order, though. Bad boys don't follow rules."

Carrie chomped on a chip. "Can you just say wish list?"

"Carrie!" Sabrina exclaimed. "You're driving us crazy with these little hints."

"Yeah," Lexi chimed in. "Come on, it's us!"

"How bad is he?" Missy wanted to know.

"The sex list is more like a wish list," Carrie shared. "To make up for what I missed with my ex. Zach's cool with everything."

Hailey pushed her sunglasses up and gave her a hard look, her pale blue eyes piercing. "This is quite possibly the worst idea I've ever heard. You simply can't go through with it."

Carrie frowned, annoyed. If she wanted a fling, she could have one. She couldn't think of a single good reason not to. "Why not?"

"Because you're a good girl," Hailey explained in a patient voice. "This will get messy with hurt feelings, and guess who's going to feel that hurt the most?"

"Her," Ally said, pointing to Carrie.

Hailey dropped her sunglasses back in place. "Yes. I know you, Carrie, you have a sensitive loving heart."

Carrie clenched her jaw, biting back the sharp remark that immediately came to mind. *Do I have to be a bitch to have fun?* She knew Hailey had good intentions. It was just that Carrie had finally gotten up the courage to go for it and she wanted her friends to be happy for her, not hold her back. She spoke in a carefully controlled tone. "I can handle a fling."

"You should get to know him," Hailey insisted. "Give him a chance to get to know you and make something real."

"But—" Carrie started.

"I say this out of love," Hailey said, reaching over and giving Carrie's arm a squeeze. She lifted her fingers, probably full of sunscreen, and discreetly wiped them on her towel. "I don't want to see you get hurt."

"I hate to say it," Ally said. "But Hailey's making a lot of sense."

Carrie pasted on a smile. "Thank you for the warning, but I'm fine with something temporary. I *want* that. And even if I wasn't fine with it—" she held up a finger "—which I am, it doesn't matter because he's heading overseas first chance he gets and I'm staying here for grad school. No way I'm taking a pass on my teaching assistantship with full tuition coverage just to follow some guy to who-knows-where."

"What happens after you're through with the list in a week or two and he's not overseas?" Hailey asked. "What if you run into him with the guys or around town?"

"I'll be polite," Carrie replied tightly.

Hailey spoke in a gentle tone. "But you might have your happy ending if you'd just give him a chance." She meant the whole romantic thing—everlasting love culminating in a wedding. The idea of being *forever* trapped in a relationship made Carrie's stomach roll. People changed, not always for the better.

Missy, a tough redheaded woman who never sugarcoated anything, put her two cents in. "Marriage isn't for everyone. It was a bad fit for me. You go for it, Carrie. Enjoy yourself."

The women dove enthusiastically into a debate over marriage and what it meant—an opportunity for happiness or a lifetime of hard relationship work. Carrie ignored all that, instead gazing serenely at the lake, reveling once again in post-bad-boy bliss. But then Hailey asked a question that triggered Carrie's automatic good-girl guilt.

"What if you end up hurting him?"

She hadn't given any thought to it because he'd seemed okay with everything. Finally she said simply, "He said he didn't want a relationship."

Hailey let out a long sigh. "Fine." She turned to the group. "So no volunteers for Ethan?"

The women were quiet. No one was eager to be set up by Hailey. Give her a little encouragement and she kept going with the hard-driving persistence that worked so well for her business. People's love lives were a bit trickier.

Hailey pulled a pink baseball cap out of her tote and

pulled it low over her forehead. "I will simply have to give Ethan extra attention myself."

"This oughta be good," Missy muttered under her breath.

"What?" Hailey asked.

"I said it'll be good for him," Missy said.

"And Josh!" Ally put in, which had them all cracking up because it was exactly what was on their minds. Josh Campbell, the bartender and manager of Garner's, had previously been a paid escort for the many weddings Hailey planned. When that arrangement went down in flames, they'd begun a hilarious frenemy one-upmanship that escalated from spicy peppers slipped into nachos (Josh's move), rumors of an affliction that caused impotency (Hailey's move), to running out of Hailey's favored mojito ingredients (Josh's move), to rumors of Josh's tiny banana (Hailey's move), to rumors that Josh was the one who got away. Poor Hailey, that last one was Josh's extremely effective move that everyone in town believed due to their palpable chemistry. Carrie and her friends all thought the frenemy thing was a cover for what Josh and Hailey really wanted—each other.

Josh would not take it well if he had to watch Hailey cuddle up to his friend Ethan. Maybe this would make Josh step up and finally make the move they all suspected he wanted to make on Hailey. And that Hailey secretly longed for.

Hailey shoved her sunglasses back on. "Josh can kiss my ass."

Or not.

5

———

Zach strode through Curtains & More, telling himself he hadn't really lied to Carrie by not explaining he was actually a respected anthropologist and not a bad boy. It wasn't like she'd asked what he did for a living. But it was a point of pride for him that he acted honorably, always honest, always keeping his word. A twinge of guilt had him gritting his teeth as the words he'd heard so many times as a kid rang through his head. *He's a bad seed. You can't trust him. Sneaky, a liar and a thief.* His parents' reputation had stuck to him. They'd been in organized crime. They weren't the muscle; they were the brains. His dad died before Zach was born. His mom, he remembered. She loved him, played with him, and taught him stuff. At three she taught him how to read, at four she taught him basic addition and subtraction using gummi bears, and at five she taught him "life skills." Namely how to pick locks, break a window without damaging your hand, and how to blend in a crowd. She left him at six with a friend for what was supposed to be a week and never returned. After two weeks, his babysitter took off for places unknown with her boyfriend, leaving him alone. He'd wandered to the corner store, stole a hot dog from the case and ate it and shoved another one in his pocket for later. But then he got greedy and stole some gummi bears.

Social Services picked him up. That was his first foster home.

He ran away so many times no one wanted to keep him. A runaway who regularly stole food and cash was a pain in the ass. He'd used all his "life skills" in running away, looking forward to the day when he found his mom and could tell her all about it. That day never came. At nine he landed in the same foster home as Ethan, who told him to quit being a stupid runaway because his basketball team needed a tall kid. That was when he met the Campbell brothers and their dad, Joe, in the Police Athletic League. He ran away once more a month later, but by then Joe had his back. It was Joe who tracked him down, helped him get the answers he needed about his mom, and let Zach know he didn't have to run away anymore because he was now home with his new family. Zach was smart enough to know when he'd lucked into a good thing. Besides, his mom had died attempting a jewel heist. Sounded like something out of the movies. Except real life wasn't that glamorous. Someone else got to the jewels first. When she tracked them down to a drug cartel in Mexico, she'd attempted to steal the jewels with some backup muscle. None of them made it out of there alive. He liked to think she did it as a way to secure a future for the two of them. The alternative—greed—just pissed him off.

He stopped in the curtain rod section, looking for some of those tie things that held curtains open. He wanted thick velvet for Carrie's Jane Bond fantasy. Yeah, he'd figured that one out. "Call me Bond. Jane Bond." Pretty obvious she wanted to try some girly light bondage. See? Even if he did leave out a small occupational fact, he was actually doing an honorable thing, keeping her safe and protected while she experimented. Seriously, was he just supposed to let some random asshole she met in a bar tie her to the bedposts and do God knew what to her? This bad-boy ruse was a noble calling for him. In some ways, you could say he was her knight in sexy armor.

His mind wandered back to the day before, Carrie on top, her face an expression of pure feminine bliss as he held her by the hips, controlling her movements, making her take more and more, pushing her past the first orgasm to a deeper one that had her screaming his name. He'd flipped her under him so damn fast, driving hard and deep, no holding back, and she'd loved it. Fuck. He felt himself getting hard. He looked to the ceiling, trying to think of anything but that. Okay, maybe his intentions with her weren't completely noble. He'd always held back in the bedroom, trying not to be too aggressive, too rough, but with Carrie he could be himself. She'd welcomed his natural aggression from that very first night when, in a haze of lust, he'd lost control. His usually carefully choreographed moves of slow seduction deserted him when she bit his neck hard enough to sting and then tried to climb his body, urging him to take her. He ripped her panties and took her fast and furious right up against the wall, pounding into her as her shouts of ecstasy rang in his ears. *Yes! Yes! Yes!*

Great, now he had full-on wood.

"Can I help you?" an elderly white-haired woman wearing a red Curtains & More smock inquired.

He shifted slightly so he wouldn't be brought in on an indecency charge. "Yeah. I'm looking for—" he cleared his throat "—velvet curtain ties."

"Oh, you have to buy them as a set with the curtains. Right this way."

He followed the woman to the adjacent section.

"What color, dear?" she asked.

"Doesn't matter."

"Well, what color are your walls?"

A rare heat crept up his neck. "I got it from here, thanks."

"Oh, well, okay. I'm Jean if you need anything else. I'll be right over there straightening the hand towels." She pointed. "See, right across the aisle."

"Thanks," he muttered.

As soon as she left, he started feeling up the curtain samples, looking for the right thickness and softness. Sure, he could've used some rope from the much more manly hardware store or even a couple of his ties, but he wanted something that wouldn't chafe Carrie's delicate skin. It was his first time initiating a woman into sexual pleasure and he took that honor seriously. He found a deep blue velvet that felt right, grabbed the set, and headed for the register.

Damn, a long line. He stared at the curtains, hoping she'd be available tonight. The more he thought about Carrie and her "traditional" ex—translation: controlling repressed jerk—the more he thought she needed the role play of bad boy, naughty girl to fully experience the passion she craved. It was abundantly clear to him that she was a good girl trying on the naughty-girl role. Not only did she have a naturally sweet demeanor, even when she claimed to be "pissed off," but she'd also taken the time, the first night they'd met, to have a frank discussion of his medical history, previous partners, and favored birth control on the drive over to his apartment. A very responsible good-girl thing to do. She then informed him that the minute his pants were down, condom had to be on because she couldn't wait to have him inside her.

Don't think about it.

He was never going to get rid of this woody if he kept thinking about naked Carrie. He pictured her in that sexy purple dress she wore when he'd first met her at Garner's. Okay, now this was just pissing him off. There was no way he wanted her approaching another guy in a bar, looking for a willing participant for her wish list. *He* was willing and able. Case closed. The best part was, neither of them were truly vulnerable as long as they played a role.

All of that led him to the conclusion that he was still an honest man, acting honorably in both word and deed. And, damn, he couldn't wait to tie her up.

Carrie didn't care if it made her look too eager, she texted Zach on her break during her shift at the hospital on Monday. So what if they hooked up yesterday? She had a lifetime of deprivation to make up for.

Carrie: *I get off work at nine. You around?*
Zach: *Yup.*

A man of few words, but who needed words for hot alpha sex?

When she got home that night, she took a shower and used the vanilla body wash she knew he liked. She also had grapefruit and lavender, but she figured she'd stick to what worked. She took the time to do her hair and makeup and put on her decadent new matching black silk bikini-style panties and pushup bra set. Her underwear drawer was neatly divided into the work side—plain white cotton bras and panties—and the pleasure side—silks and satins and lace. Not that she'd ever worn this sexy stuff for Edward. He'd hated the one time she'd bought some sexy lingerie, said she looked like a prostitute and it was beneath her. She'd felt such shame, but no more. This beautiful stuff was all new for her new life.

She slipped her little black dress on and then, the final touch, the slutty black heels. Zach had a thing for the heels, leaving them on her that first night. Until she'd accidentally stabbed him in the back with one of the spiky heels. Still, they were by far her sexiest shoes.

She grabbed her phone and saw she had another text from Zach. *This wish list is a monogamous thing.*

She pressed a hand to her heart, touched by the unexpected sweetness. His focus was solely on her. And since hers was likewise, she texted back. *Duh.*

She had no need to find another man when Zach was already doing such a fantastic job. They'd already accomplished three of the seven things on her list—wallbanger, oral sex, and woman on top. At this rate they'd be finished in less than a week. Unless she asked for a repeat of some stuff. He *had* offered two weeks.

She stuffed her phone in her purse and rushed out of the bedroom. She didn't want to think ahead like that. Too much good-girl behavior for her taste.

Ally wolf-whistled from the sofa, where she was watching a hospital drama that drove Carrie crazy with the medical inaccuracies. Geez, hire a consultant so the audience could have an honest authentic view of hospital work. "Sexy mama!" Ally hollered, waggling her eyebrows.

"Thank you! Heading to Zach's."

"You spending the night?"

Carrie halted. "Oh, I don't know."

"You did last time. Text me so I don't worry if you don't come home."

"I'm sorry. Did you worry last time?"

Ally waved that away. "Yes, I worried, but then I figured you were so overdue, you probably pulled an all-nighter."

Carrie hesitated. Now this was awkward. She didn't want Ally to worry, but she didn't know if she'd pull another all-nighter or if she'd finish and be ready to go. This fling stuff was so complicated. Finally she just decided not to worry Ally. "I'm spending the night. Don't wait up." If she came home early, no big.

"Have fun and don't tell me about it." Ally returned her attention to the TV. "It's too depressing with my drought situation."

"Ally."

"La-la-la, can't hear you."

"Bye."

She stepped outside and the door next door popped open. Great. It was her eighty-year-old neighbor Larry, aka the lucky accidental recipient of her very explicit sex list. His white hair was neatly combed and he wore a red silk robe loosely belted with an abundance of white chest hair showing. His legs were scrawny and bare. "Hello, Larry. How're you?"

"Wonderful!" He smiled widely and stepped out to the outdoor hallway. It was a warm August night, so she didn't mention he should put some clothes on. He tucked a thumb into his robe pocket, jutting one hip in a casual male-model pose. *If only.* "Nice night. Going to meet a fellow?"

"Just meeting a friend. Bye!"

"You know, Carrie, sometimes the young men of today—"

"Good night!" she exclaimed loud enough to drown him out. She made her escape, rushing down the stairs and to her car. She'd have to move to ever get over the awkwardness with Larry.

She made the short drive to Zach's place, not wanting to walk the three blocks in heels in the dark. She parked on the street and made her way to the front door, putting a little swing into her hips in an attempt to get past elderly flirting and back into her womanly mojo.

She rang the bell and waited. A few moments later it swung open and her mouth went dry, her heart pounding.

Zach stood there looking impossibly sexy in a gray T-shirt that stretched tight across wide shoulders, faded blue jeans, and bare feet. But it was his eyes that held her in thrall, filled with a dark hunger that made her feel both desired and nervous. Like he was about to pounce on her.

"Hi," she said much too loudly.

One corner of his mouth curled up in a small smile. His voice was gravelly. "Come in."

She took a quick breath and stepped inside on wobbly legs.

He watched her with hooded eyes. She clasped her icy hands together. Why was she suddenly so nervous? Then she realized she was stone-cold sober. Never mind that she was sober the morning after their first time together. That had felt more natural and relaxed somehow. Shifting from work to the encounter with Larry to hot sex wasn't as easy as she'd hoped.

"You, uh, have any wine?" she asked, heading toward the sofa.

"No."

She set her purse on the floor next to the sofa and sat.

He stood, still a distance away. "You change your mind about your list?"

"No. Absolutely not." She forced herself to stand and cross to him. He watched her approach but said nothing. She stood toe-to-toe with him and lifted her chin. "I'm ready when you are."

He slid a hand under her hair and squeezed the nape of her neck before leaning close to speak near her ear, the words hot against her skin. "I figured out your whole list, naughty girl." He bit her earlobe and tugged it between his teeth.

A hot shiver ran through her and her hands found their way under his shirt. "You did?"

He pulled back and met her eyes. "Yeah, I did, Jane."

She dropped her hands, disappointed he couldn't even remember her name. "It's Carrie."

His fingers encircled her wrists. "Jane *Bond*."

"Oh! Yes. Ha-ha." She was about to ask what he thought that Jane Bond business meant, but before she could get out the words, he drew her arms behind her back, capturing her wrists in one hand in a tight grip. Her pulse skittered, her breath coming faster.

His other hand held her by the chin, his dark eyes glittering with intent. "Tonight you're all mine, Jane."

"Yes," she whispered.

His lips met hers in a hard demanding kiss. He pressed on her chin, opening her mouth and thrusting his tongue inside. She moaned, her body arching up to meet him, straining to get closer. His hand left her chin, tangling in her hair, his mouth devouring, hungry, overwhelming. She was lost in his taste, his spicy male scent, light-headed with lust. She needed more, wanted to grab him and pull his hardness against her softness, anything to ease this aching need, but he still held her tight, her wrists clamped in his large hand. His other hand left her hair and cupped her suddenly between the legs. Her soft moan was swallowed by his mouth. His fingers slid the damp panel aside and then they were inside her.

He tore his mouth from hers. "You're so wet for me."

"I know," she cried as he stroked her inside, making her tremble.

He released her suddenly, turned her and smacked her ass lightly. "Bedroom." When she didn't move right away, a little startled by the sudden change, his arms wrapped around her from behind. He spoke in a husky whisper. "So I can tie you to the bedposts."

She moved forward, more because Zach's arm banded around her waist and he walked with her than of her own free will, her stomach jumpy, her heart racing. This was one of those things she'd felt like she should try—getting tied up.

Now she wasn't so sure. She didn't know him that well. What would he do to her? What if she couldn't get loose? She'd put it last on the list, but he was such a bad boy he was going all out of order.

Her voice came out shaky. "M-maybe we should start with something else on the list."

He stopped and turned her to face him, studying her for a long moment. "Like what?"

"Sunday drive?" she blurted, extraordinarily relieved to have an out. Car sex sounded a lot safer than getting tied up.

He jerked his head toward the door. "Let's go."

6

―――

Zach walked Carrie to his pickup truck, fully aware he was being accommodating, which was not a bad-boy thing to do. What he should've said was, "Babe, get in my bed and spread your legs, or get out." But he'd felt her nervousness, seen a flash of true fear in those baby blues, and he couldn't do it. He knew she had no reason to be afraid of him, but she didn't know that. Not yet. That he was committed to her achieving the best possible experience with her wish list was only a reflection of his true goal—keeping her safe from random strangers. Not because he had a soft spot for her.

They got to his truck in the parking lot behind the apartment complex and he purposely didn't open the passenger door and help her in like he normally would. Too gentlemanly. Instead he pinned her against the side of the truck and kissed her. Not gently. Then while she was still standing there, breathing hard, eyes glazed with lust, he swaggered over to the driver's side.

Yeah, he was disappointed about not tying her up. It was the one thing on her list he was psyched about. What did it say about him that he loved to dominate in that way? Nothing significant, he decided, climbing into his truck and starting it. All within the realm of normal male behavior, given the invitation to do so. Hell, if there weren't some aggression in the male of the species, the population would have dwindled long ago, everyone sitting around chatting instead of getting down to business. He was tuned into the primal, thanks to his academic background, and he embraced it.

He checked that her seatbelt was on and then pulled onto the main road, heading for the park where he'd spent plenty of Saturday afternoons playing basketball with the guys and plenty of high school nights up on the ridge making out with a girl. This "Sunday drive is sometimes bumpy" would go further, obviously Carrie wanted to give car sex a try. Easy enough.

"Where're we going?" she asked, sounding considerably calmer than earlier.

"Park."

"So you really figured out everything on my list?"

"Yeah."

"How do I know you figured out everything correctly?"

"You'll have to find out—" he paused long enough to keep her on edge "—the *hard* way."

She giggled nervously, which told him he'd pulled off the attitude. "Oh."

The park was a short drive, technically closed now past eight p.m., but there were no gates preventing entry. He didn't anticipate any company either since it was a Monday night. Carrie sat up straighter and peered around at the mostly dark park. Just a few streetlights on the main road. He drove past the basketball courts, the playground, baseball fields, and hooked a right, climbing up to the ridge, where he parked on the gravel, facing the overlook.

He turned off the truck and listened. Dead silence. Just them and the night sounds—cicadas were carrying on with their mating calls. He turned and looked all around. They were alone.

"C'mere," he ordered. "Straddle my lap."

She took off her seatbelt and tried, but her dress seemed to halt her progress and she bounced back into her seat. "My dress is a little too tight."

"No such thing," he said, yanking her dress up to her waist and then guiding her over into position. He stifled a groan as she cradled his cock through damp panties. She smelled like vanilla and sex and he'd been ready for this moment since she'd stepped into his apartment in a tight little black dress and high heels that made her hips sway and sweet ass tilt back for his greedy hands. He told himself to go slow. Each experience was new for Carrie. Anyone could fuck hard and fast. He wanted to make it good for her.

He slid a hand to the nape of her neck, under her soft hair. He was about to slowly pull her in for a kiss when she beat him to it, slamming against his mouth. Jesus. She kissed him roughly, urgently, eagerly, her fingers tunneling through his hair. He thrust his tongue inside, loving the taste of her, sweet and sexy. She sucked his tongue gently and he lost control. Need like he'd never felt before spiked through him. He gripped her hair with one hand, plundering her mouth, his other hand gripping her ass. She made needy little mewls into his mouth. He gave the side of her panties a tug.

She tore her mouth from his. "Don't rip them. They're my favorite."

"Next time don't wear any."

Her mouth slammed against his, her tongue darting inside. He held her by the jaw, taking over the kiss, his cock throbbing painfully against the confines of his jeans. He grabbed her hips with both hands, trying to lift her, desperate to get himself free and buried deep inside her, but she was clinging to him, her legs squeezing the sides of his. He gave up, instead working his fingers under the side of her panties and thrusting inside.

She threw back her head. "Yes!"

Oh, God. Hang on, hang on, make it good for her. He sucked on the cord of her neck and gave her another finger, angling the way he knew would make her crazed. She got real noisy then. He let her ride for a while, getting more and more turned on by her throaty cries, probably one thrust was all it would take to get him off.

"Now, now," she said. "Inside me." She leaned back and fumbled with the button on his jeans.

"I got it."

A hard rap sounded on the driver's side window, making him jump and Carrie yelp. Fuck. A flashlight shone in his eyes, probably a cop. He quickly shifted Carrie back to her seat, where she wiggled down her dress.

"Open the door," a male voice ordered. "Police."

"Omigod," Carrie whispered.

He opened the driver's side door and the flashlight shone on Carrie's face. She probably couldn't see anything but the glare of white light. "You okay, ma'am?" The much softer tone with a hint of a smirk told him who he was dealing with —Ethan. His honorary brother and pain-in-the-ass cop friend.

"Yes, Officer," Carrie replied. She was probably too startled to put it together yet. Ethan did sound very official.

"Would you like assistance out of this vehicle, ma'am?" Ethan asked.

"No, I'm fine, thank you."

"You," Ethan barked, shining the flashlight in Zach's eyes. "Out of the truck and keep your hands where I can see them."

Zach gritted his teeth.

Carrie rushed to his defense. "Officer, please, this was all my idea."

"Sir, please step out of the vehicle," Ethan ordered quite convincingly.

"It's my fault!" Carrie cried.

Zach let out an exasperated breath, stepped out of the truck, shut the door, and faced Ethan in full alpha mode—feet spread apart, hands on hips, deadeye stare. That Ethan was the one who taught him how to stare down trouble might've made it less effective.

Ethan squared off with him, getting in his face like he was about to tell him off. Then he smirked. "She's watching."

"Make it good."

"I'll keep the flashlight where she can see us both," he said under his breath. Then he straightened and barked, "You know I'm within my rights to haul you out of here for trespassing. Signs are clearly posted saying the park is closed."

"Arrest me," he challenged.

Carrie opened the passenger-side door and poked her head out. "Everything okay? I can vouch for him."

They both turned to look at her.

"Ethan?" she asked. Carrie knew all the guys through Mad Campbell.

"Hi, Carrie," Ethan said casually. "I'll work this out with Zach. Get back in the truck."

"Ethan!" Carrie chided. "You scared the bejeezus out of me!"

Zach bit back a smile. Even when she was mad, she was just so damn cute.

Ethan dipped his head. "Ma'am, just doing my job."

"Ugh! Men!" She got back in the truck and slammed the door.

Ethan shook his head, smiling and enjoying his part in this outdoor venture a little too much.

"You're such a cockblock," Zach snapped.

Ethan chuckled. "What're you doing taking her to your old high school make-out spot? You've got a fucking bed now."

He spoke in a low tone. "She wanted a little thrill from, you know, being out in public. I'm helping her out with some edgier stuff."

Ethan laughed. "You?"

"Fuck you."

Ethan slowly shook his head. "I can't believe she picked a professor of all people for a little edgy sex."

Zach flipped him the bird and turned to go.

Ethan grabbed his arm. "All right. Don't get your tweed in a bunch. I've got some ideas to help you out."

Zach shook him off. "I don't need ideas." He had a very specific wish list to follow.

Ethan ignored that. "Give her elevator sex. She works at Eastman hospital. Take her in the service elevator."

Zach studied him for a moment. "And how do you know about this service elevator?"

Ethan smirked. "Had to review the security tapes once. Sex central, man."

"Ass."

Ethan snorted. "Hey, maybe a sex tape."

"I'm going now, unless you're planning to arrest me."

Ethan socked his arm. Hard. "Just trying to help you out."

Zach socked him back. Harder.

Ethan chuckled. "Taking her to your old high school haunt. I mean, really. Use some imagination."

"You done?"

"Yes, Professor. Carry on your merry way."

He turned on his heel and stalked back to the truck, pissed at Ethan's implication that he was a wuss. No more accommodations. Carrie wanted bad boy and that was exactly what he'd give her. Put up or shut up time.

Carrie wasn't sure what to say after that weird almost "Sunday drive" interrupted by Ethan. Zach was silent, looking kind of pissed as he drove them out of the park.

She broke the silence in an attempt to put a pleasant spin on the evening. "Well, I'm just glad you didn't get arrested for trespassing." Ethan had scared the crap out of her. Now that she thought about it, he probably recognized Zach's truck. "He was just messing with you, wasn't he?"

Zach grunted in response.

"So maybe we could just drive to another private spot."

"We're going back to my place."

"Oh, okay. How about we—"

"Carrie, I don't take requests. You want this, you go back with me and we do things my way. You don't, I'll drop you off at your car."

She gulped. That was abrupt. Also a little thrilling. He sounded so badass.

"You mean Jane Bond?" she asked.

"Yeah."

"I'll have to think about it."

"Time's up once I park."

She didn't have to think long. She was still revved up from earlier and the unexpected cop encounter had added a bit of danger. Now that everything had turned out okay, she was actually feeling really good. Charged up and alive.

"Okay," she said. "I'll be Jane."

He reached over and gave her upper thigh a small squeeze, his long fingers curling intimately around the inside of her leg. Her body responded with a pulsing throb.

She let out a shaky breath. He wasn't much for conversation, but he got his point across in a direct primal way. His thigh squeeze told her two things—he was happy with her decision and he was also reassuring her that it would be a good time. Somehow he knew exactly what she needed to hear.

When they got back to his place, he put a hand on the small of her back and guided her directly to his bedroom. Once inside, he shut the bedroom door, grabbed her and pinned her against it. The breath whooshed from her lungs and her stomach dropped. He pinned her wrists over her head and kissed her, his leg nudging hers apart and pressing close. The jumpiness in her belly shifted to a low ache.

He released her wrists and guided her arms back to her sides. "Don't be nervous." His voice was low and gruff, his eyes hot on hers. "I'll keep you safe."

Goose bumps shivered along her skin. "Okay," she whispered, the word muffled in the fabric of her dress flying over her head.

He swore, his eyes glued to her now exposed cleavage. "I can be gentle," he muttered, more to himself than her. He slid the bra straps down her shoulders, then softly traced the line from her neck to shoulder, bringing more goose bumps racing over her skin, then across her collarbone and dipping into her cleavage. He groaned, undid the front clasp and sent the bra flying. He cupped her breasts with both hands, his thumbs stroking the hard peaks and then pinching them. She melted against the door, her eyes closing, surrendering to the intense pleasure.

He nipped her neck roughly and her eyes flew open. He nuzzled the side of her neck, his soft beard grazing her sensitive skin, heightening the sensations of his warm lips and sharp teeth, kissing and nipping, the intensity building as his hands roamed all over her. She moaned softly, aching for more.

"Take off your clothes too," she said urgently.

Instead he slid her panties down and off. Then he clamped a hand around her wrist and pulled her to the bed. He yanked back the covers, and then he was kissing her hungrily, guiding her down, under him. She wrapped her arms around him, eager for the closeness again, for his kisses that made her mindless with passion and pure need.

He peeled her arms off him, slid her to the center of the mattress, and then grabbed two blue velvet ropes from the nightstand. She swallowed hard, her stomach fluttering, every nerve ending tingling with anticipation. He didn't give her a chance to get too worked up, though, instead leaning down and kissing her, gentle and coaxing, showing her he could be gentle. And then just brushing his lips against hers, making her sigh.

"I'm gonna tie you up now." His gravelly voice made her toes curl. "You'll like it."

He lifted her right wrist above her head, wrapping the velvet rope around it and tying it to the wooden headboard with lots of convenient wooden slats to tie things around. "Give a tug."

She did. It was loose. She could probably slip out of it easily. Well, was she going to do this or not? Yes, she decided. All or nothing.

"You're going easy on me," she said. "Don't."

He grunted a masculine sound of satisfaction and tied it tighter. Then he grabbed her other wrist and tied that one. She tugged, truly at his mercy now. A hot shiver ran down her spine as his eyes met hers, gleaming with stark hunger. Fierce. Raw. Animal.

He snapped his teeth at her. She squeaked.

He bit her lower lip gently and then sucked. "Your safe word is good girl."

She clamped her mouth shut. She would not be admitting to that.

A slow sexy smile crossed his features before he leaned in, tracing her lips with his tongue and then delving deep. The kiss turned ravenous. Yes, this was what she wanted. Mindless passion. He shifted, kissing down her throat and then cupping her breast before his mouth closed around it, sucking hard. This was not gentle and she didn't care. She was throbbing, hot and wet and aching for his touch. His teeth closed over her nipple and she cried out.

He lifted his head. "Did you say something?"

She shook her head.

"Sure?"

"I'm sure." She tugged at her ties, wanting to grab his head and make him get back to her breasts or lower. Please God, lower.

He leaned up to inspect her ties, running his fingers under the ropes. "How're your wrists? Not too tight?"

"Argh!"

He met her eyes and lifted a brow. "Argh?"

She tried to flail one arm and merely wiggled it. "Get back to business."

He rolled her nipples and tugged on them. "You're not in a position for that kind of order, naughty girl."

She let out a sigh of relief as his mouth closed over her other breast, sucking hard, that tugging achy feeling returning, a direct line to her sex.

He released the suction with a pop and looked up at her. "Don't pull too hard on the ties, no matter what I do. Got it?"

A full-body shiver ran through her. "Yes." She opened her legs in invitation.

He shifted much lower, settling between her legs, staring at her exposed sex. "Beautiful." He slid one long finger inside her and met her eyes. "I'm gonna push you, but you'll like it."

She let out something between a gurgle and a moan.

He dropped a kiss on her sex. "Ready?"

"Yes!" He was being so strangely sweet considering she was tied to his bedposts and he'd just promised to make her so crazy she'd want to pull at her restraints.

That was the last coherent thing she said. His fingers were magic—stroking, pinching, thrusting inside her, bringing her to the edge of release. She tensed, panting, about to explode when he stopped and kissed her inner thigh. And then kissed his way up her body to whisper in her ear, "Let me do one more thing and I'll give it to you."

"Please," she moaned.

He kissed his way back down her body, this time working her with his lips and tongue and teeth, making her body bow up off the mattress, keening with need. The tension coiled within her, higher and higher. Oh, God, yes. Please, please, please.

He lifted his head, whispering something that sounded soothing.

She could barely focus. "What?"

He levered back up her body, thrusting his finger in her mouth, which she sucked, tasting herself, erotic and hot. Her hips lifted in shameless entreaty. He whispered in her ear, "One more thing. Then you can come."

She moaned. His wet finger stroked down her throat. His lips followed the trail of his finger down her body between her breasts, down her belly, stopping just short of her throbbing, aching center.

He blew softly across her sex, stroking her lazily up and down, over and over, murmuring praise as she moved to his rhythm, needing so much more. She yanked at her ties, wanting to smack him or jump on him. Something to ease this never-ending ache.

"Easy," he soothed, sliding his fingers inside her.

She let out a shaky breath. "Please this time. Please."

He stroked inside her and then shifted so his thumb was working her at the same time. Her entire body jolted as he found the G spot she'd heard about but never felt. He increased the pressure, his thumb stroking back and forth, faster and faster, his fingers stroking on the inside. She writhed with need, her hips raised off the bed, wild animal sounds escaping from somewhere deep inside.

The pressure eased as he gentled and slowed. He used his other hand to push her hips back on the mattress. "Easy, relax."

She looked to the ceiling and let out a stream of curses.

He cupped her sex and held it. "Now you're getting it."

She looked at him, ready to scream. "What am I getting?"

His voice was low and gruff. "You're mine to do as I please. I say when. I say how much. No choice but to go with it."

Her breath hitched, her skin fever-hot, every nerve ending electrified. He stroked her gently, lazily, and she whimpered, her legs quivering.

"Unless you use your safe word, naughty girl," he drawled.

She closed her eyes in refusal and then they flew open as his mouth closed over her throbbing center just as his fingers thrust inside her, stroking slow and easy. She was wild with need, bucking under him, but he stilled her with one large hand on her hip. She keened long and low.

All of his intense focus on her.

Everything just for her.

And she just couldn't…take…much…more.

She trembled as he pushed her slow and easy, over and over, and then she broke, shock waves of pleasure radiating from her core, shooting straight down her legs and up her torso. A full-body orgasm like she'd never felt before. She panted, her heart pounding, electrified. She had no idea she could come like that.

Finally he released her and she relaxed, limp and sated.

"One more time," he said, standing next to the bed, quickly stripping off his clothes and rolling a condom on.

She swallowed, beyond words, sure she didn't have "one more time" in her. He returned to her, lifted her legs up and over his shoulders, and thrust deep.

"Yes!" she cried.

And then he was pounding into her, rocking her, hitting just the right spot, and she was crying out in pure bliss. His hand slipped between them, stroking rapidly, and she lost it, the orgasm slamming through her, stealing her breath. He kept going, thrusting deep, hard and fierce. It was too much. The intensity. Her body clenched around him, her heart pounding as hard as he was pounding, wild, primal, lost in shock waves of sensation all controlled by him.

"Zach!" she cried out, her head thrashing from side to side, the only movement she could manage.

He held her by the jaw and cheek, keeping her still and their eyes locked on some deep primitive level that made her tremble. Then he thrust deep and she exploded with a harsh gasp, stunned, light-headed in a haze of pleasure as he pumped for his own release and finally let go.

A long moment later, he withdrew and lowered her shaky legs to the mattress. She was drenched in sweat, his and hers, in a shocked state of wonder that she could ever experience those kinds of orgasms—a full-body radiating pleasure, a hard slamming explosion and then another. She'd never known. He'd made her come before but not like that.

His big hands framed her face and he kissed her gently before untying her wrists, kissing the underside of each tenderly, and then pulling her into his arms.

She felt safe, protected, cherished. She'd never experienced anything like it. Passion and tenderness. Who knew a bad boy could do all that?

7

———

Carrie ended up spending the night. It was an unspoken thing, as in, she dozed off after all the Jane Bond excitement. She'd woken up a couple of hours later and started feeling him up. He must've been awake because he'd immediately responded, kissing her breathless and then saying in his gruff and growly voice, "I'm gonna take you sideways. You'll like it."

He was so confident, she totally believed him. She'd faced him on her side, scooting closer. "Tell me what to do."

"Roll the other way."

Then he took over, taking her sideways like he'd said. And she'd liked it.

She'd conked out shortly after.

Now she rolled to her back, all wrapped up in the blanket. Zach wasn't in bed. The scent of coffee and something cinnamony reached her. She definitely had to stay for breakfast. It would be rude to rush home to dry toast.

She stretched lazily, a satisfied smile spreading across her face. Zach was kind of like a sex teacher. He told her what he was going to do, told her she'd like it, and then made it happen. And she was the eager student. She liked when he went off list too. After taking the leap of faith to get tied up, she was ready for anything. She trusted him.

She let out a happy sigh, rolled out of bed, quickly dressed, and went to brush her teeth.

~

Zach held a secret satisfaction that Carrie had texted to come over again the very next night after he tied her up. That meant she'd enjoyed it as much as he had. This sexual compatibility on top of personal compatibility was rare in his experience. She didn't mind that he wasn't overly talkative or touchy-feely. Two complaints he'd heard repeatedly from ex-girlfriends. She hadn't seemed to mind that he always slept on the couch, needing to sleep solo. Or maybe she didn't notice. She was usually out cold by the time he was done with her and he did wake up before her. Whatever. It worked.

He never had to hold back with her in or out of bed. He could be himself. Except for his bad-boy ruse. But that wasn't so bad, was it? They were both happy with the arrangement. They enjoyed each other's bodies. They enjoyed eating break-fast together and talking about cooking. Mostly him answering her questions on how he made stuff without a recipe because she didn't cook much. In any case, their time together felt right. Natural.

The doorbell rang right on time. He opened it and took in his mate. He gave himself a mental shake for slipping into anthropological mode there. Carrie wasn't *his* and definitely not as permanent as a mate. But, damn, she was sexy as all hell in a light blue tank top with matching short shorts and the biggest smile on her beautiful face.

He couldn't help but smile back. "Come in."

He backed up a few steps to make room for her.

She dropped her purse, ran, and leaped into his arms. He caught her instinctively. Her arms and legs wrapped around him and she kissed him all over his face. Dangerous warmth spread through his chest, a soft emotion that would bite him in the ass if he let it show too soon. Timing was everything.

He slid his hand over her pretty ass and between her legs, her heat igniting raw desire in him. Primal instinct triggered, he walked straight to the bedroom, his arms full of sexy woman.

Carrie was only on day five of wanton abandon with Zach when she realized they'd nearly completed the list. She was addicted to what he made her feel—a passion and freedom in the bedroom she'd never known existed. She was a little worried, though, because she'd actually considered missing her every other Thursday book club meeting just to be with him. Her friends would be there for her long-term; Zach wouldn't. But she didn't want to waste one minute of her time with Zach, so as a compromise, she invited him to meet her at Garner's for the usual after-book-club drinks. He'd inquired into the male-female ratio, not wanting to be the focus of the women with questions into their arrangement, and when she told him he'd be the only guy, he'd promptly invited Ethan. Zach didn't hold a grudge over Ethan messing with him on their disastrous "Sunday drive" in the park. No harm done was how he put it. In any case, Hailey was thrilled because it worked perfectly with her plan to flirt with Ethan and clear his name as not-a-sex-addict.

"So, ladies, what did we think about *Rescuing Hannah*?" Hailey asked the group. The women, nine in all, sat in a circle of chairs in Something's Brewing Café. It was a cozy meeting place with deep red walls, hanging light fixtures with golden sconces, dark wood tables with matching chairs, and dark wood laminate flooring. The coffee and pastries were to die for. Usually they arrived just before closing to get their drinks and snacks before their reserved private meeting time. It was a win-win for the local owners of the shop because they also owned Book It, connected to the café, where the women spent most of their book dollars.

Rescuing Hannah was their first romantic suspense, a darker story than they normally read and had scared the daylights out of Carrie.

"It was good," Mad said, tossing her dyed fire-engine red

hair out of her eyes. "Lotta good action." Mad was a black belt, a tough woman, the youngest and only girl from the testosterone-filled Campbell family.

"It scared the crap out of me!" Lauren, a sweet second-grade teacher, exclaimed. She was a good friend of Carrie's. "Every time I heard a scratching noise I thought it was the serial killer at my window. And I have cats! There's always some scratching noise somewhere."

"It scared me too!" Carrie said at the same time as Sabrina.

"Jinx!" Sabrina said, socking Carrie in the arm.

"Ow." She rubbed her arm.

The women were divided on whether or not it was truly scary or just suspenseful.

Hailey interrupted the debate. "I liked that Hannah played a big part in her own rescue after she was captured."

The women murmured agreement. That had been pretty awesome.

Hailey went on. "And then when she and Colt were on the run and hiding out in the cabin, it was so steamy..." She trailed off because the women promptly launched into a discussion of Colt as a book boyfriend and what he had that other book boyfriends didn't have. Not all of them made the cut for book boyfriend.

Carrie found her mind wandering back to Zach, who was right this minute across the street at Garner's with Ethan. Ally had driven her to book club so she could ride home with him and she knew it wouldn't be long before she and Zach would bail. The chemistry between them only intensified the more they did together. She'd expected it to ease up, at least a little. There was no book boyfriend who could compare to what Zach did for her. In just five short days he'd made up for so much of what she'd missed out on with her ex. Hard to believe she'd only known Zach for less than a week when she felt so comfortable with him. She'd fought back the urge to ask him questions about himself, knowing it would make her get too attached. It was the only way to protect her tender heart. She didn't talk about him with her friends either. Not that anyone knew much about him, they'd all just met him for the first time at his welcome-home party, except Mad, who'd grown up with him. His sweet smile came to mind, bringing a rush of warmth. He showed it rarely, but when it came out, it just bowled her over. She let out a swoony sigh, remembering the last time he smiled like that, this morning when she—

"Carrie?"

She straightened. "Huh? What?"

Hailey exchanged a look with the other women. "I said are you still with us?"

"Yes. Why?"

"Because Mad asked you how realistic the medical scene was after Colt was shot and you just let out a happy sigh."

Carrie flushed. "Sorry. Yes, it was realistic. The author definitely did her research."

"How's Zach?" Hailey asked.

"You're with Zach now?" Mad asked. She'd missed their beach day when they'd discussed him, and Carrie had been on a nonstop work-fuck-sleep schedule ever since.

She considered how to answer. She knew, above all, Mad would take her honorary brother's side over anyone else, even a friend. If she told her it was just a fling, she'd hassle her on why. In a way, it was true that she was with Zach now, even if there was a time limit on it.

"Yes," Carrie said.

"For her sex list," Ally put in.

Carrie whipped her head toward Ally. "Would you stop calling it a sex list? It's a wish list."

"A wish list of sex," Ally returned with a grin.

"Don't tell me any more," Mad said with a grimace. "I don't want the squicky details."

"Good." Carrie fought the blush creeping up her neck. "Because I don't want to share anyway."

"That was fast, though," Mad said. "He's only been home for a week."

"Carrie threw herself at him," Lauren said. She'd had a front-row view of the event since Carrie had been with her right before she claimed her womanly mojo at Zach's welcome-home party.

Carrie glared at all of them, daring them to judge her, but the other women just looked fascinated. Probably because they knew she was usually more reserved around men. She'd been picky, not wanting to settle for more ho-hum. She'd wanted a fling with the alpha bad boy of her fantasies as a way to push the envelope, to find the passion she'd craved. And she was proud that she'd had the courage to go after him.

"He's whip smart," Mad said. "Worked so damn hard—"

Carrie interrupted. "Did you and Park set a date yet?" Blatant topic change but she wanted to keep Zach a mystery.

"Yeah, next June," Mad muttered, deflating with wedding talk. She wanted to get married, even wanted a nice wedding at Ludbury House, the mansion in Clover Park where a lot of weddings were held. She just didn't like all the work of planning it.

Hailey spoke up in a perky voice, turning to Mad. "You just relax. I'll handle all the details."

Mad jerked her chin in acknowledgment of Hailey's superior wedding planning abilities. Well, it was Hailey's job, after all.

Hailey reached over and squeezed Mad's hand, who flushed bright pink, but didn't pull away.

Hailey addressed the group. "Well, ladies, are we ready to wrap up and head over to Garner's for drinks?"

The women answered in a chorus of *hell yeah* that had them gathering their purses, chattering like always as they headed out, down the sidewalk, and across the street. Even though some of the members had recently married or gotten engaged, they always made time for their sisterhood. Who knew bonding over romance could forge such strong friendships?

When they got to Garner's, the bar was already crowded with couples and several guys drinking beers and watching the Sox game on the TV mounted over the bar. Since it was way past dinner, the adjacent dining area was nearly empty. Her heart kicked into double time the moment she spotted Zach, his back to her, sitting with Ethan at the dark cherrywood bar. She took in his thick shaggy hair that was luscious to thread her fingers through. His wide shoulders and broad back that stretched the fabric of his dark green T-shirt and that cute ass in faded jeans. It wasn't like she didn't see him every night. She stopped by after her shift at the hospital (after a shower). Now that she'd gotten over her initial reserve, each time she showed up at his place, she leaped into his arms and peppered him with kisses. There was just nothing better than knowing he was waiting for her, willing to give her everything she desired.

The truth was, just looking at him made her feel lit up inside. But that wasn't because of dangerous emotion that would leave her feeling hurt. It was more like her body remembered all the wonderful orgasms he'd given her, so it lit up in anticipation of more. At least she really hoped that was why.

She caught Hailey watching her and nodded once in a gesture of *this is no problem. See? We're two consenting adults with a short-term mutually beneficial arrangement.*

Ethan said something that had Zach turning toward her. He didn't smile, but his eyes were locked on hers, the intense focus telling her she was the most important person in the room to him. It was how he made her feel every time he looked at her. Delicious heat speared through her, a flutter low in her belly, electric energy shooting down her legs, urging her to run and leap into his arms.

No, she couldn't do that here in front of everyone. She had to play it cool. Especially in front of Hailey, who'd been very clear about her concern for the temporary nature of their relationship. She slowly, casually made her way to him and he watched her approach with hooded eyes.

When she reached him, she used his shoulder for leverage, went up on tiptoe and kissed his temple. "Hi!"

He held her chin and kissed her gently on the lips. "Hi, Carrie," he said in the deep honey voice that made her melt.

"You want my seat?" Ethan asked.

"Hi, Ethan," she said cheerfully, drawing attention to the fact that she wasn't embarrassed in the least at being caught almost having car sex and that she found him perfectly acceptable to talk to on a social occasion. *He's not a sex addict, people!* "I'm good with standing."

"Sure?" Ethan asked with a smirk. "Seems like maybe you and Zach might want to—"

"Oh, we see each other every night," she assured him. "He just met me here to save time. We're heading out after this."

Ethan's brows shot up. "Is that right?"

"Leave it," Zach told Ethan in a low tone. Then he picked her up and settled her onto his lap.

She heated everywhere with his casual display of strength and what almost felt like possessiveness. Zach took alpha to an exhilarating level. His arm banded around her waist and he shifted her to face the bar. He pushed her hair back, his lips grazing her ear as he whispered in his deep erotic voice, "What do you want to drink?"

She shifted slightly to meet his eyes. "I usually get white wine."

His expression was intense—serious and focused. "Is that what you want?"

It suddenly felt like the question meant so much more. Do you want more of the same? Do you want to try something a little more dangerous? And then the message she got loud and clear, that she suddenly realized she'd felt with him from day one, bounced through her brain—*live it up, Carrie. I'll keep you safe.*

This was why she had zero inhibitions with him. Why she leaped into his arms, knowing he'd catch her. How was it that a bad boy made her feel so safe?

"You pick," she said and faced front.

He leaned toward her, his soft beard grazing her cheek. "Ever try tequila?"

"Nope."

"You'll like it."

She nodded, valiantly attempting to look cool even as she went damp between the legs. "You'll like it" was the phrase he used right before he rocked her world. The message was always the same: *I'm gonna fuck you like this. You'll like it.*

"I'll take one too," Ethan said. "It's been a helluva week."

Zach waved the bartender over. Josh jerked his chin and held up a finger to wait while he served some guys beer on tap. Josh was the oldest Campbell brother, along with his identical twin, thirtyish with dark brown hair that curled a bit, brown eyes, muscular bod. He was a former paratrooper in the army and kept fit. He was dressed casually in a faded black T-shirt that showed clearly defined muscles with ripped jeans. Carrie liked him a lot. He was always laid-back, charming, and flirty, except with his number one frenemy Hailey.

A few minutes later, Josh had her, Zach, and Ethan all set up with shots of tequila, salt, and limes.

Hailey appeared, standing close to Ethan. "Ooh, I'll take one too."

"Nope," Josh said.

This was to be expected. In keeping with their never-ending frenemy war, Josh never let Hailey have a drink other than water. It was a drastic measure, considering they were all regular patrons of the bar that Josh managed, but Carrie had to admit the punishment fit the crime. Hailey had squashed the impotency rumor she'd started by implying Josh had a tiny banana. Denying Hailey drinks was the only revenge Josh had been able to inflict short of whipping it out to prove his manliness. He'd also spread the news far and wide that they used to be a couple and Hailey was just bitter that he was the one that got away. But that wasn't nearly as satisfying as continually denying her drinks.

"Come on, Josh," Ethan said. "Have a heart. The poor woman looks parched."

Hailey let out a tinkling laugh. "Oh, Ethan, you're so funny." She touched her neck, met Ethan's eyes and then looked away and back. Classic flirty move. "Maybe I could have a taste of yours," she said in a husky voice.

Ethan's gaze turned speculative, taking Hailey in from her perfectly smooth strawberry blond hair to her perfectly made-up face to her perfect body in a formfitting gray tank dress that ended mid-thigh with tan gladiator sandals with ties that wrapped up her calves. She always looked like she just stepped out of a glossy fashion mag.

"I'll get you your own damn tequila, princess," Josh grumbled and served one up, slamming the shot glass on the bar in front of Hailey. Some tequila sloshed over the side.

"You need to get laid," Ethan told Josh.

Josh's dark eyes were locked on Hailey. "I get plenty of action."

Hailey held Josh's gaze, licking her hand, sprinkling it with salt, and licking again. Josh stared at her mouth. She threw the shot back and sucked the lime. "Woo! That is good stuff!"

Josh swore under his breath, averting his gaze. "You're cut off."

"C'mere," Ethan said to Hailey. "Give my hand a lick and I'll give you my shot too."

Hailey licked her lips and then ran her fingers through Ethan's short dirty blond hair. "I don't lick just anyone, but you—" she paused dramatically and finished loud enough for the entire bar to hear "—are a fantastic candidate for a classy lady like me."

"Fucking A," Josh muttered, snatching Ethan's shot and tossing it back himself. His dark eyes flashed with irritation and heat. Probably because he was pissed that he was turned on. Carrie was much better at recognizing the signs of male desire now, thanks to Zach.

Josh slashed his hand through the air at Ethan and Hailey. "You're both cut off." He stalked to the other side of the bar.

Hailey went right back to flirting with Ethan, who seemed receptive. Guess that worked. Carrie stopped watching the two expert flirts when Zach lifted his hand near her mouth and spoke in the deep gruff voice that never failed to make her hot. "Lick."

Her insides clenched, her heart sped up, and she licked. He added salt. She licked again, grabbed the shot, downed it and coughed like crazy. Omigod, it burned, it burned.

"Suck the lime," he said.

She did, her eyes watering. She turned to see if he was

laughing at her inexperience, but he merely studied her in his observant way.

"How you feel now?" he asked.

She smiled, suddenly giddy. "Good." Loose and languid, she relaxed back against her man. Her temporary man, she reminded herself. His own drink remained on the bar.

She shifted to look at him and offered her hand. "You want to have yours now?"

"Depends."

"On what?"

"You want to stay here for a while, then I'll take the shot." His gaze smoldered with an intensity that gave her a shiver of anticipation.

"And if I'm ready to go?"

"Then I'll give you a ride back to my place right now. No shot." He whispered in her ear, "Primal, Carrie. You'll like it."

She shivered. "Yes, let's go." It was one of her wish list items—animals are primal—and she couldn't wait to see how he'd interpreted it.

He lifted her off him without another word, tossed some bills on the bar, and guided her to the back parking lot, his hand on the small of her back, the touch bringing a flare of heat.

He helped her into his truck, got in the other side, and they were off. Heading for another exhilarating ride. And when she floated back to earth from the heights of ecstasy, she landed once again safe in his arms.

8

Zach made his way to the bed and flopped down on the mattress after a round of shower sex that lasted so long the water ran cold. "Squeaky clean is best" had been fairly easy to interpret. Actually, her whole list had been easy to figure out once he'd understood the deeper meaning of what she really wanted. For him, it didn't matter what they did as long as he didn't have to hold back. She didn't want unnaturally gentle. She wanted take charge. She wanted him. For the first time he got just as much pleasure giving pleasure as he did taking his own. Her responses brought him immense satisfaction as he watched her blissful states from wonder to awe to amazement. In those moments, sex became an almost spiritual thing. A new and awesome experience for him.

He glanced over at Carrie already in bed, staring at the ceiling with a look of pure feminine satisfaction. She frequently just lay there, quietly reliving the experience. She'd shared that with him the first time he'd been concerned at her long silent state. Most women liked to talk after.

She had an intensely sensual side, not much for conversation, which suited him perfectly. He was the same way. Mostly they texted in small doses, like from Carrie repeatedly: *You home?*

And him: *Yup.*

He always made sure he was home in time to hook up with her. He liked being her bad boy, liked her a lot, but he had no idea where to go from here. She'd gotten under his skin much faster than he normally let anyone in. His lone-wolf nature hadn't deterred her. Not that they'd spent any time together in the traditional sense of dating with getting-to-know-you conversations, but he knew the important things. He knew what she felt like—soft satin. What she tasted like—vanilla and sexy woman. What she sounded like—sweet, caring, open. If things progressed further, he'd tell her about the professor thing. He was actually a little surprised it hadn't come up already. Carrie never asked him about himself, only about cooking. She must not have asked around about him either. What did that mean? Was this just about sex for her? Because for him it wasn't.

It had to be more. Every night, the moment she stepped into his apartment, she lit up at the sight of him, ran, and leaped into his arms. No one had ever lit up just at the sight of him. He replayed those nightly reunions in his mind when he was running or driving or supposed to be working on his book—bubbles of pure incandescent joy. Fleeting, maybe. Temporary. They were technically at the end of their agreement—he'd gone through her entire list, even stalling by adding some of his own stuff in between. His chest tightened.

He wasn't ready to let her go.

He turned his head, watching her staring at the ceiling, her lips curved into a small smile. The tension in his chest eased a bit because he'd made her happy.

He hadn't thought they could get through the list so quickly in only a week. Carrie worked the one to nine p.m. shift at the hospital and showed up at his place after, spending the night and staying late into the morning. He still slipped out to the sofa after she fell asleep. And she still hadn't noticed. He was glad; his ex had hated that he was a solo sleeper. He supposed it was his lone-wolf nature because he'd never been able to sleep with someone cuddled up against him. Women tended to be cuddlers.

He stared at the ceiling and ran a hand through his damp

hair, exhausted from his week. He got a workout both day and night. Usually when Carrie was busy at work, he sat at the computer, trying to come up with a better outline for his book. He couldn't get past the first third. Even his title "Society Against State: Geopolitics Surrounding Indigenous Nations of Southeast Asia" sounded too academic. His work didn't translate as easily as he'd hoped for a nonacademic audience. He'd stopped and started several times, yet it kept turning into PhD dissertation part two. His brain just wouldn't bend in another direction no matter how hard he tried. So he ended up running, working out, driving around, visiting the guys. Anything that would take him out of his head and jog things around in there. Maybe it would help if he unpacked all the boxes full of books and binders of field-work and reviewed everything. Hell, who was he kidding. The minute Carrie realized he was a professor of anthropology, she'd dump him. She wanted a bad boy. Considering his previous hard-core honesty, pretending didn't bother him as much as he'd thought it would. The bad boy-naughty girl role play was the most relaxed he'd ever felt with a woman.

She *had* invited him for drinks with her friends. Gaining acceptance of a potential partner with friends was important in a relationship. Though maybe the invitation to drinks had just been her way of seeing her friends for their standard get-together while still having the option to pursue her real goal —more passion with him. They were both addicted to what they had in the bedroom. The more sex they had, the more sex they wanted to have.

He'd be around for a few more months. Maybe she'd agree to keep seeing him. It would be torture to run into her around town, knowing he had to keep his distance. He scrubbed a hand over his face. *Selfish.* He had to think of her feelings. He would definitely be taking that Singapore opportunity, leaving right after Christmas to get settled there. The fellowship was highly prestigious and could lead to his choice of job later at a top university. He was fairly certain he'd get it, only a matter of waiting for all the paperwork to clear through the committee. It pained him to admit it, but deep down he knew it wasn't fair to lead her on with something long-term knowing he was leaving the country.

He lay there for several more minutes, agitated with his warring desires to keep her close or push her away for her own good. Dammit. He knew the right answer. He wouldn't be leading another woman on with a relationship only to ruin things in the end.

He rolled to his side and was struck all over again by her beauty. Not just a surface thing. Beautiful inside and out. So pure of heart it made his own heart ache with longing for just a small piece of it.

He pushed a lock of hair back from her face. "Carrie."

"Hmm?"

"I went through your whole list." He waited to see if she wanted out.

She turned to him and beamed. "We crushed it! Let's go a full two weeks and repeat everything!"

Yes! "Cool." The reprieve drained the tension right out of him.

She rolled into him and started kissing his neck, her hands roaming all over his chest and then lower.

He felt himself getting hard again. Two weeks was for the best. He needed to buckle down and get focused on his book. The university was paying him for this year off and he needed something to show for it. He couldn't just sex, sex, sex all the time like an animal. He stifled a groan as Carrie's hand closed around him.

"Carrie," he croaked because she'd gotten really good at stroking him just the way he liked. It was a damn feat of strength that he could speak at all.

She stilled her hand and looked at him with some concern. "Yes?"

"Two weeks is the max I can do. It's not you. I just don't do long-term."

"Never?" she asked softly.

He couldn't tell if she was hurt or just clarifying out of curiosity. It didn't matter. The important thing was to be clear. He cradled her face with one hand, brushing his thumb over her cheek. "Never," he said and then kissed her gently to ease the harshness.

She kissed him back passionately, her hand gliding up and down the length of him, and any harsh truths seemed forgiven. He relaxed, revved and ready for round two. She shifted, grazing her cheek against his beard like a cat rubbing against him, still stroking him to blue steel. Then she grabbed a condom and rolled it on him.

The moment her hand shifted off his throbbing cock, giving his brain some much-needed oxygen, he asked, "What should we repeat first?" He wanted to make sure he repeated all her favorites in the time they had left. He'd liked everything on her list, but was in the mood for one item in particular—animals are primal. His accurate interpretation: animals are primal, humans are animals. Ergo, take me doggy-style. It was the most natural position if you looked big picture at all the animals.

"Mmm, surprise me," she said.

"How's number five?"

Her bright blue eyes sparkled with good humor. "Don't ask; just do, bad boy."

He couldn't help his grin at her turn of phrase. "Don't ask; just do. You sound like Yoda."

"You sound like a man who's not getting number five."

He flipped her to her stomach and lifted her by the hips, taking her in one hard thrust. He groaned long and low.

"Yes!" she shouted like usual when he took charge.

She arched back into him and his brain shut down, primal need taking over. Fuck academics. He *was* an animal.

Carrie woke that night with a gasp, eyes wide open, heart pounding. Oh, thank God. It was just a dream. She was still in Zach's bed. She'd been dreaming she showed up to her parents' fiftieth anniversary vow renewal ceremony when it suddenly turned into her wedding to her awful ex Edward. He'd said all the vows and the minister didn't care that she said nothing, the marriage went through. Final. Stuck forever. She'd tried to run but got nowhere, running in place, Edward's hand clamped around her wrist.

She rolled over, searching for Zach, and found only an empty bed. Where was he? She checked the clock on the nightstand. Four a.m.

She rolled out of bed, wrapping the blanket around her bare shoulders, and padded out to the living room. He was asleep on the sofa. She stopped in front of him and stared in the dim streetlight filtering through the living room window. His legs were too long for the sofa and he had to sleep on his side, knees bent to fit. Why would he sleep out here when he had a king-size bed in the other room? Shit. It was because of her. That first night she'd been so worn out, she'd let herself fall asleep in his bed. And then he'd made her breakfast the next morning and it was all so wonderful, she kept doing it. She should've asked if it was okay to spend the night or, better yet, forced herself to wake up and drive home. Guilt stabbed at her, making her chest tight. He'd given up his bed for her without complaint.

But was it really so bad to sleep with her? They were so intimate with each other in other ways. Her throat tightened, suddenly hurt that he'd rather squish onto the uncomfortable sofa than sleep with her, even though she knew she had no right to be upset. This was probably his way of not getting too attached when they were only temporary. Her stomach rolled. Okay, she'd fix this. All of this fling stuff had been her idea, so now she'd make sure he went back to his bed, where he could stretch out and be more comfortable, and then she'd drive home.

She sat next to him and ran her fingers through his thick soft hair. "Zach?"

No response.

"Zach," she said louder, "let's get you back to your bed."

He didn't stir. She nudged him a few times, but he was out cold. He was much too big for her to get him there on her own. She didn't want to go back to his bed alone, the nightmare wedding still fresh in her mind. She slid in next to him, lying on her side, her back to his front, and pulled his arm over her waist. There. His body warmed hers, his spicy male scent surrounded her, and she completely relaxed, falling into a deep sleep.

She woke in the early morning when Zach maneuvered her onto the sofa and himself off. "Hey," she said softly, "I don't want you to have to squish on the sofa."

"You fall asleep before me." He stood, looking down at her in his undershirt and red and black plaid boxers. "I don't want to disturb you."

She sat up. "Your legs are too long for the sofa. I'll go home after so you can have the bed."

He cupped her jaw and grazed his thumb over her cheek. "I'd never kick you out of bed."

Her breath caught, surprised at the sweetness. "Okay, then, you can sleep *with* me."

He dropped his hand. "I'm just used to sleeping alone." He left, heading toward the bedroom, probably for the connected bathroom.

She flopped back on the sofa, pressing a hand to her aching chest. What did she expect from a fling? It wasn't like they did anything but have sex and eat breakfast together. This wasn't a relationship, which was fine. Neither of them wanted that. He didn't do long-term. She was glad. The last thing she needed was to lose herself again, all wrapped up in a man, supporting all of his dreams while neglecting her own.

A short while later, she heard Zach in the kitchen. Probably getting the coffee started. Lately she'd been noticing more and more of the considerate things he did. She told herself he would do them for anyone. He was still every bit the bad boy she'd hoped for, back from a mysterious no man's land, a world traveler with survival skills, a skilled sensual lover that left her wrung out, limp and sated. He probably had a checkered past too. All the guys that hung out with the Campbell family did. She hadn't pressed Zach to share intimate details and he hadn't offered. Further evidence that this was a fling. Neither of them was interested in true intimacy.

He probably didn't think twice about having coffee ready first thing when she woke. Or leaving an extra towel and washcloth for her on the dresser. Or cooking for her.

Or sleeping on the sofa so he wouldn't disturb her sleep.

Had she been all wrong about him?

He stepped out of the kitchen and pulled his undershirt off in a quick two-handed move. That got her attention. Tanned skin, defined pecs and abs, those muscular wide shoulders. She sat up, hoping the boxers would drop next.

He inclined his head toward the bedroom. "Shower with a twist. You'll like it."

She shot off the sofa. It didn't matter what he had in mind, all of his ideas were fantastic. And she not only liked it, she *loved* it.

He waited, his eyes eating her up as she approached him, completely naked, feeling beautiful and sexy under his gaze. At the last minute, she pivoted toward the bathroom, just out of his reach. He caught up to her and swatted her ass. She let out a small squeak of surprise before he scooped her up, tossing her up and over his shoulder. He was definitely bad in the best sense of the word.

Much later, they made their way to the kitchen. They both guzzled water and then helped themselves to the waiting coffee. They'd turned sex into an Olympic sport and had to rehydrate regularly.

"Take a seat," he said before turning to get breakfast stuff out of the refrigerator.

She did, bringing her coffee with her. "What're you making?"

"Omelets."

So, okay, eating breakfast together every morning was kind of domestic and relationshipy, but she couldn't help herself. He was such a good cook. And he *wanted* to cook for her. She couldn't be so rude as to let all of his culinary efforts go to waste.

She sipped her coffee and thought about her parents' upcoming fiftieth anniversary celebration. Yesterday her mom had warned her that Edward was bringing his twenty-year-old fiancée. Her mom had offered not to invite him when they'd first started planning the event, but Carrie had said it was fine. She planned to be polite and work around him. Besides, it would've made things awkward for her parents on this special occasion. Edward and his parents had shared most special events with their family—Christmas Eve parties, Fourth of July, summer vacations. She'd missed him last Christmas while she'd been at her friend Claire's wedding and had skipped the summer activities, but this renewal ceremony was a big deal, so she sucked it up. It wasn't every day your parents celebrated fifty years together.

Too bad things hadn't worked out with her and Edward like everybody had hoped. She'd told her parents they'd broken up because Edward had strayed. She'd left out the kinky sex he'd sought elsewhere to keep her "pure." God, she loathed Edward, the cheating liar. He'd deprived her of passion while he'd been doing all sorts of depraved sex stuff with…whoever. Thank God he'd been religious about using a condom. She'd had a thorough STD screening, anyway, once she'd realized what he'd been doing.

But now that she knew he'd be there with a young fiancée at his side, she had cold feet. The renewal ceremony was technically past the agreed upon two weeks for her and Zach, but she'd dearly love to show up there with her sexy badass boyfriend to show Edward she'd moved on and was doing just fine.

The delicious scent of breakfast cooking—omelet with ham and green peppers—reached her a short while later. It would be hard to miss out on all of Zach's delicious breakfast food once their two weeks were up, but that was the deal. Maybe she could keep it going just a little longer.

She took a deep breath before saying as casually as she could manage, "I know our two weeks will be up next Saturday, but would you mind if we extended it by one day?"

Zach turned from the stove to look at her. His dark hair was still damp from the shower with comb lines from where she'd combed it. So hot. He let her do whatever she wanted to him. "Why?"

She hated to ask, but it would make things so much easier with her ex. "Next Sunday is my parents' fiftieth anniversary. They're renewing their vows in a ceremony on the beach and…" She winced, hating to bring up Edward.

"And?" he prompted.

She sighed. "My ex Edward will be there. His parents are close friends of my parents. I was hoping you'd go as my date."

"Your parents invited him, knowing he hurt you?" His voice, gruff and curt, told her what he thought of that. She warmed, knowing he was on her side.

"They offered not to invite him, but I didn't want to make things awkward. Edward's family has always joined ours for special occasions."

His lips formed a flat line, studying her for a long moment.

"I admit I don't have the most honorable of intentions. I want to make him jealous and show you off."

His lips curled in a slow sexy smile. "Nice."

"So you'll do it?"

"Yeah." He turned back to the stove.

She shifted uncomfortably, imagining Edward saying something unkind and Zach striking back or maybe even kicking his ass! He had that alpha thing going on. She didn't want any kind of testosterone showdown on her account. Not that Zach was in love with her. They both knew this two-week one-day fling was about sex.

"Uh, Zach, please don't say anything to him, okay? No matter what he says, let me handle him."

He didn't reply. Just kept cooking barefoot in his sexy blue T-shirt and faded jeans.

"I mean it," she said firmly.

He shifted the omelet to a plate and crossed to her, setting it in front of her. "If you could handle him, you wouldn't need me there."

"Forget it," she muttered, annoyed at how well he could read her. She didn't *need* him there, but she *really* wanted him there. She could feel Zach's eyes on her as he continued to stand by her side.

"Carrie." His tone was surprisingly gentle.

She didn't reply, just sliced into a corner of her omelet. She didn't want him to feel sorry for her and she definitely didn't want to share about Edward's stupid fiancée because she was afraid she'd end up all teary. That could've been her and, even though she'd turned him down when it *was* her, it still stung. Edward and this other woman couldn't have been together very long. Edward took *six years* to propose to her and then not until after she'd dumped him. His proposal was a last-ditch effort to get her back. She took a small bite of omelet and groaned. Effing delicious.

"Just watching you eat is an erotic experience," Zach said gruffly.

She found herself smiling. "So's watching you cook. Guess that worked out."

He cupped her head and dropped a kiss on top of it. "I'll be there."

A warm glow filled her, her throat tight with emotion for his understanding and support. Before she could manage a thank-you, he'd returned to the stove. Feeling better, she ate her delicious omelet and, a short while later, he joined her with his breakfast, taking his seat across from her.

"You want me to be extra badass in front of your ex?" he asked, slicing into his omelet. "Black leather jacket, swagger, swearing a blue streak, maybe a switchblade in my back pocket." He widened his eyes. "Bit of the crazy eyes?"

Her hand went to her throat. Her sweet senior citizen parents would die! "Maybe not that far."

He inclined his head. "Your call."

"I love your badass look just like it is. Wild hair, beard, and all that hard muscle."

"Funny, I was going to say the same thing about you." He grinned and took a bite of omelet.

"Not quite the same," she said, reaching over and stroking his beard.

He finished chewing before saying, "I'm overdue for a trim. I'll get cleaned up in time for the anniversary thing."

"Don't do it on my account." No matter what he looked like, her parents were going to be curious about him. "Maybe we should get some of the basic info on each other so we're not caught off guard when you meet my parents."

He ate some omelet and took a sip of coffee. "Shoot."

"How old are you?"

"Thirty-four."

"Middle name?"

"Edward."

"No!"

He smiled, his eyes crinkling up at the corners. "Kidding. Zachary Joseph Harrison."

She threw her napkin at him and he laughed, handing it back to her. "I'm twenty-six," she said. "Carrie Elizabeth Young."

He ate some omelet and spoke around it. "You're too young for me, Carrie Young."

"Ha-ha. I can take you."

He met her eyes with a devilish gleam. "Sure can."

She blushed at the reminder of all the intimate things they'd done. "So you know I'm a nurse and you're…" She waited for him to fill in the blank. She'd spent all of her free time with him this week, mostly not talking. She'd held back her curiosity, but now that he was sharing, she was dying to know more.

He sipped some coffee and studied her over the rim. Just when she thought he wasn't going to answer, he said, "Currently unemployed."

"Because you just got back from Indonesia?"

"In part."

"And what did you do there?"

He sliced some omelet and chewed, taking his time answering her. Finally he said, "Checking out the islands, hiking and camping in the forest."

"No wonder you look like a wild mountain man. Is that how you make money? Travel tours of the islands?"

He resumed eating.

She stared at him for several long moments while he said nothing, his sole focus on his food. She gave him that, he was probably hungry. Finally she couldn't wait any longer. "Zach? Is that what you do?"

He lifted his coffee mug to his mouth, muttered, "Yeah," and took a sip.

"Cool! I'd love to take a tour with you."

He set his coffee down and met her eyes directly. "I'd love for you to see Indonesia. Beautiful scenery, beautiful people."

"When do you go back?"

He stared at the table for a moment and then met her eyes. "I'm heading to Singapore next for a two-year gig. Right after Christmas."

"Oh." She forced a smile. "I'm starting grad school in a couple of weeks for my master's in nursing. I'm going to be a certified pediatric nurse practitioner. I was lucky enough to get full tuition coverage with a teaching assistantship."

"Congratulations. How long is your program?"

"Two years."

Their gazes locked for a moment of shared recognition of what that meant. Two years, two different continents, two very different career paths.

Finally Zach broke the silence, saying quietly, "Sounds like we both have a two-year plan though you're getting a semester's head start."

"I guess so." He'd still be gone for two years. She stared at the table, her fingers tightening into a death grip on her mug. She forced herself to relax her fingers, lifted the mug to her lips, and realized it was empty. Caffeine was not what she needed right now. She nearly vibrated with tension, blindsided by a separation across the world. She swallowed down the emotion that had no place here. She had no claim on Zach, had worked hard to keep things light. So, she got her wish, fate intervened to make them an impossibility. She'd get through this ordeal with Edward and then say goodbye to Zach. Her gut churned. No, that wasn't right. Zach had been good to her and he didn't deserve being used as a buffer for a situation he had nothing to do with.

She lifted her eyes to his. "You don't have to be my date for my parents' anniversary. It was selfish of me to want you there. I'll deal with Edward myself."

"Too late, already invited me."

"Zach."

"Carrie," he growled with a note of finality.

She lifted her palms. "Okay, okay. Thank you."

He grunted and returned to eating.

She debated if she should warn him about the kind of man he'd be meeting. They were as different as two people could be, which she was happy about, but she didn't want Zach to be caught off guard. Edward was a snooty intellectual, something he'd worked at. His parents were down to earth.

"Edward is a brilliant doctor," she said. "A brain surgeon."

"So? Even smart people can be stupid." He finished his omelet in one big bite, his teeth snapping together.

"Zach."

He chewed and swallowed. "What?"

"That was sweet."

"Nothing sweet about it. Edward was clearly stupid to miss out on all you have to offer." He cleared his throat. "I mean, you have so much passion and all."

She blushed. "You're the one who's so passionate. I'm just trying to keep up."

His eyes were warm on hers. "It might just be us."

The word *us* hung in the air between them, shimmering like a tiny star of promise. She looked away first, a little off balance at the shifting sands of what she thought was a solid understandable thing. A fling. Temporary. Necessarily shallow so no one got hurt.

Two different continents.

She marveled for a moment that their paths had ever crossed at all. Her chest ached to think about missing out on everything he'd shared with her. The way he'd taken her list seriously and brought her such pleasure. She'd always be grateful for that. She grabbed his coffee and took a sip to ease the awful tightness in her throat. He watched her drink but made no comment. She set the mug back in front of him.

"Do you have a suit?" she asked brightly, eager to move the conversation to a safer topic. "I'll be wearing a dress. My dad will be in a tux. My mom actually fits into her wedding gown."

He sipped his coffee. "I can scrounge one up."

"It's not a problem if you can't. Just a nice shirt and pants will do."

"I won't embarrass you."

"Oh, no. I'd never be embarrassed. You're the hottest guy I've ever been with."

He grinned.

"Not that I've been with a lot."

He stopped smiling. "Just me and your ex, I remember."

She ran a hand through her hair. "I'm sorry. I'm just…I guess I'm a little worked up about the whole thing. You know, seeing Edward again after all this time. And his fiancée. Apparently she's young and beautiful."

A small smile curved his lips. "So are you."

She sucked in air. That was such a sweet thing to say. The second sweet thing this morning. And he was a man of few words, so when he used them, they meant something. "Thank you."

He jerked his chin and took another sip of coffee. Something that felt less like lust and more like pure affection built in her. Strong affection like she wanted to hug him. Not to feel him up either. Just to hug.

He set his mug down and watched her steadily.

She blurted the first thing that came to mind. "I feel really bad I've been taking your bed every night."

He shook his head. "Not a problem."

"I'll go home after so you can stay in your bed, where you'll be more comfortable."

He met her eyes with a hard look. "I don't want you out alone in the middle of the night."

She returned his hard look. "And I don't want you squishing yourself onto a sofa your legs are too long for."

"I'm fine."

"No, you're not."

He leaned back in his chair. "I can't believe our first fight is us trying to out polite each other."

"A fight would imply a relationship."

He rubbed the back of his neck. "I don't know what this is."

"Me either." She kept telling herself it was a fling, but it was beginning to feel different. The air felt charged, the conversation rife with hidden meaning. Somehow things had shifted this morning when she'd invited him to her parents' anniversary celebration.

He brought the coffee mug to his mouth and spoke behind the rim. "Let's not screw with what's working."

She bit her lip, his casual reply stinging more than it should. "No, of course. You're right. Just—" she swiped a hand through the air "—leave it alone." She couldn't keep the bitterness from her voice.

He set the mug down. "I mean *you* said two weeks."

"You offered two weeks," she returned. "I just agreed with it."

"What're we even fighting about?" He stood and stacked the plates. "I'll sleep in the bed if it makes you happy. Okay?"

"Fine."

"And don't think you're leaving alone in the middle of the night either." He stacked the silverware on top of the plates. "We'll both sleep in the bed."

She tilted her head back to meet his eyes where he stood next to her. "I *said* fine."

"Good," he growled. Then he leaned down and kissed her breathless. He pulled away, studying her for a moment before grabbing the dishes and heading to the sink.

She sat there, her head spinning, wondering what the hell just happened.

9

___

Zach sat at the kitchen table with his coffee and watched Carrie rinsing the breakfast dishes, still a little rattled by their spat. He checked her out in her simple dark gray tank top with matching dark gray shorts as she bent to put a plate in the dishwasher. She had the most delicious cleavage, the prettiest ass. She liked to match her clothes, tops and bottoms, even down to her underwear.

And she'd invited him to meet her parents.

It didn't take an anthropologist to know what it meant to take someone to meet your parents. Clearly Carrie wanted to take what they had to relationship level. Now that the pressure was off with Carrie occupied at the sink, he could analyze the situation. She had feelings for him. He'd hoped, but he hadn't known until that moment.

He did some quick calculations of when exactly he'd be in Singapore and when Carrie would graduate from her program and realized that he'd be away two solid years right in the middle of her program, which followed the school year so was actually more like two and a half years. It was too long a separation for where they were at.

But there were real feelings here on both their parts. That meant something. Right?

Would it be so bad to give it a try in the few months before he left? Wouldn't it be better to grab whatever happiness they could now?

He wanted to try. If it worked out, maybe she'd be willing to postpone grad school for a couple of years and go with him. Whoa. That was a ridiculously big jump ahead. Especially coming from him. What if he ruined it like all his other relationships? What if he truly was too much of a lone wolf to ever pull off the intimacy needed for a successful relationship? If he got her out to Singapore and things fell apart, there was no guarantee she'd have a full tuition teaching assistantship waiting for her back home. Full tuition coverage was always a competitive thing. Limited dollars to go around, everything depending on who you were up against in that particular academic year. Or…he could pass on the Singapore opportunity. No, that would be foolish. He was at the point in his career where the fellowship could give him a significant boost in the world of academia. He might even be able to land a job at NYU or Yale afterwards, close to Carrie. Long-term view, if they had a long-term, definitely pointed to him taking the fellowship.

She hummed to herself as she worked, and a rare sense of contentment washed over him.

Maybe if he really thought through the *right* way to do a relationship, not his usual way of letting things unfold naturally, which somehow always meant falling apart, it could work. Surely his academic background could help him. Why hadn't he thought of that before? It worked wonders for the initial dance of courtship, why shouldn't it work for the advanced stages?

He shifted to anthropologist mode, examining the underlying meaning to Carrie's invitation. It wasn't just an invitation to a relationship now that he thought about it. Gaining approval of a chosen mate with family and community was a crucial step to a lasting union. Her request for protection from Edward further signaled she understood Zach was a fit protector. Zach knew his size, deep voice, regular displays of strength lifting Carrie, as well as his natural aggression in the bedroom had made that abundantly clear. His gift of breakfast each morning showed—on a primal level, the most important level—that he was a good provider. The only thing left to prove his value as a mate was a display of physical strength with a rival for her affection. Wrestling would be ideal. He had experience with the best—Ethan, Josh, Jake, and Marcus. Bonus, as a surgeon, Edward would likely be reluctant to use his fists with the risk of damaging his hands.

He briefly considered bumping his social status to be on par with Edward's medical degree by telling Carrie about his PhD. Zach could also be called "doctor." But then he thought better of it. After the anniversary celebration, he'd break the news he wasn't a bad boy, but, in fact, a respected anthropologist. Then he'd tell her how she lit up his world and he wanted to keep seeing her. He'd lay it all out logically, their compatibility, the real feelings they both had, and then he'd make a case for giving them a chance in whatever time they had left. They'd figure out the Singapore thing at a later date. Despite all evidence to the contrary—his disastrous past relationships and the terrible timing of their respective career plans—he was hopeful.

Carrie wiped her hands on a paper towel and turned to him. "All set."

He stood. "I'll drive with you to your place and walk home. I'd like to talk to Ally."

Her eyes widened. "You would?"

He understood her surprise. Before the invitation to a relationship, their boundaries were clear. He spent time with her strictly inside his apartment, no dates, no drives home. In any case, it was important he get to know and gain the approval of her closest friends. Her roommate was a key person in Carrie's friendship web.

"Yeah," he said. "We only met briefly before."

Carrie smiled uncertainly. "Well, okay, if you want to." She cocked her head. "Why, exactly?"

"I'd like to get to know your friends."

He went to the living room and retrieved her large purse with multicolored flowers from where she'd dropped it right before she'd leaped into his arms. It was their nightly ritual.

The damn thing weighed at least twenty pounds. Probably because she carried shampoo and shit back and forth from her place. He should probably clear some space for her stuff.

He crossed to her and held up the purse. "This thing is too heavy. You're going to strain your back."

She took it from him. "It's fine. I'm used to carrying a lot." She sailed toward the door and he admired the swing of her hips for a moment before catching up to her.

He slipped on the brown leather sandals he always left by the door. "You can leave some shampoo here or whatever." He straightened and gazed directly into her eyes. "I'll make room for your stuff."

She stared at him, her brows scrunched together. Good, she was thinking about the deeper meaning. He held open the door for her, locked up, and walked her down the sidewalk, one hand on the small of her back.

"Zach?"

"Yeah."

"Leaving stuff at your place feels a little different. And you getting to know my friends feels like, I don't know, something more."

He refrained from explaining the symbolism to her, not wanting to show his academic bent.

She looked up at him. "I thought you weren't looking for a relationship."

"I wasn't."

"Oh. Me either."

"Let's just see how it goes."

"See how it goes," she echoed. "I don't know what that means."

He faltered because she sounded wary. Normally he'd back off right away, but his old way had never worked out. He went for it. "You know, see how it goes. Like no artificial cutoff. Just see how things pan out." *Idiot. Get to the point.* "I really like you."

"Oh." She smiled tightly. "I like you too."

This was not going how he'd hoped. They walked to her car in silence. It was already a hot and humid August day, though it was still morning. Reminded him of Indonesia. He missed it even though he'd just been there last month. He was sure Carrie would love it there too, but it was too soon to speak of taking her for a visit, so he remained quiet.

She unlocked the car. "Zach, I'm not ready for a relationship. I think it would be better if we kept to our two-week one-day agreement. After my parents' anniversary celebration, we'll say goodbye. Of course, we'll still see each other around. As friends."

He couldn't breathe for a moment like she'd just sucker punched him in the heart. How could he have interpreted her intentions so inaccurately? Was Carrie testing him? Putting up a smokescreen to protect herself? Hoping he would stand up and declare himself before she declared herself as invested in what they had?

"Zach?"

"What?"

"Do you understand?"

"What's not to understand?" he countered. Playing it cool was his only resort. He couldn't believe he'd misjudged the situation so badly.

"Maybe I shouldn't leave stuff at your place."

"You can leave it. Take it with you when you're done."

"Are you mad?"

"No." *Yeah.* He was pissed, but mostly at himself for being arrogant enough to think he could figure relationship stuff out using his intellectual prowess. Years of failed relationships had rightly taught him he wasn't good at this stuff. For some stupid reason, he'd hoped he could power through using his brain this time. Screw it. He was missing whatever it was that made relationships work. He probably only felt so much for Carrie because deep down he knew she wouldn't want a relationship. Not because of him, because she just wasn't ready.

It wasn't personal.

He hoped.

He wouldn't ask. That way lay madness.

He got in and they made the short drive in silence.

When they got to her door, he waited while she pulled out the key. It took her forever because her purse was so stuffed. "It always seems to be on the bottom," she said.

Farther down the hallway, a door popped open. An elderly man in a red silk robe, looking like a Hugh Hefner wannabe, stepped out and gave Carrie a lecherous smile. She didn't notice, still rummaging through her purse.

Zach straightened to his full height and squared his shoulders.

"And who are you?" the man inquired, looking at Zach suspiciously.

Carrie jumped, her cheeks flushing pink. "Oh, hi, Larry. Didn't see you there. How're you?"

"Fine," Larry said. "Is this your boyfriend?"

Zach dropped his voice to the level of *back off, old man.* "I'm her *man*friend." Boyfriend sounded too juvenile. Partner didn't go far enough to keep lecherous old men from getting ideas.

Larry narrowed his eyes. "Carrie is—"

Zach cut him off. "I know exactly who she is and what she needs."

"Zach!" Carrie exclaimed.

Larry frowned. "Well, no need to be coarse."

Zach stared him down.

"Have a nice day," Larry mumbled and hustled back into his apartment.

Carrie looked up at him, incredulous. "What was that about?"

"Man thing." He made no apologies for protecting her from the likes of Larry. Or any man that looked at her with lust in their eyes. Caveman behavior? Maybe. But he embraced his inner caveman. She should know that by now. He was all about the primal.

"He's really harmless."

Zach grunted. He wasn't so sure about that and wouldn't leave it to chance.

"Found it!" She held up her key.

He kissed her, a swift hard kiss, hoping it wasn't for the

last time. "See ya tonight," he said gruffly, making sure to show zero emotion. He didn't want her to know he was worked up that she might not stop by tonight. He especially didn't like how vulnerable this whole thing had made him. He had to toughen up. Prepare for goodbye.

"I thought you wanted to talk to Ally?" She pointed toward the door.

His intention in that regard had him backing up a step. "Another time."

"Sure?"

"Yeah."

"Okay, bye." She let herself in, not seeming upset in the least while he was damn near howling.

He trudged home, heart and limbs heavy, the cold slap of reality hitting him once more because he *still* didn't know if he'd get to see her tonight.

~

Carrie sensed Zach wasn't happy with her, and the last thing she wanted was to screw up the remaining time they had together. She had no plans to extend the time beyond her parents' anniversary celebration for the simple reason that it would be too easy for one of them, namely her, to get hurt. It wasn't that Zach wasn't wonderful. He was everything she'd ever hoped for in a bad-boy lover. It was just the idea of a real relationship, of her heart so far gone that losing him would feel like a piece of her had died, she just wasn't ready to go there again. And now that she knew they were heading in two very different directions, she knew it was better to end it sooner than later.

She texted him that night once she was freshly showered in the vanilla body wash he loved and then showed up at his door, planning to pretend everything was normal. Like no awkward conversation had ever happened.

The door sprang open and Zach gifted her with one of his rare smiles that made his light brown eyes somehow warm and sparkle at the same time.

His voice was deep and low and tender. "Carrie."

"Back up." Normally he turned and walked inside with no prompting. It was how she had the room to leap into his arms.

He shut the door behind her and backed up to the middle of the living room, his arms open. She took off, leaping at him. He caught her, but this time his arms wrapped tight around her in a close hug. She couldn't even kiss him. His hand cupped her head to his chest, his other arm around her back in an unusual quiet embrace. Surrounded by his heat, his familiar spicy scent, his heart beating strong and steady under her ear, she was briefly, utterly content. Then she remembered herself. The limits of what they could have.

As soon as he loosened his hold on her head, she popped up and peppered him with kisses. His hands shifted to cup her ass, deliciously warm through her thin shorts. She kissed and sucked along his neck enthusiastically, so happy he was welcoming her back to his body. He walked with her in his arms and then her back hit cool wall. Desire spiked through her, soaking her panties, because she knew she was getting a wallbanger. One of his best moves, her feet couldn't even reach the ground in this position. She was at his mercy and she loved it.

He lowered his head, but instead of his usual rough kisses, he kissed the corners of her mouth before trailing to her jaw, lingering on her throat and then her collarbone.

"Zach," she moaned, "I want you."

He kissed her gently. "I want to take my time with you." He set her on the ground and stripped her out of her T-shirt and bra, his hands cupping her breasts, stroking over her hard nipples. She leaned against the wall, her head tipping back at the pleasure of his hands, and then he dropped to his knees, taking her breast into his mouth and sucking deeply. It was like a direct line of pleasure to her sex. She ached fiercely for what she knew he could give her. She wasn't used to waiting this long for him to get down to serious business. She tugged at his hair, trying to pull him away and redirect him, but he merely switched to the other breast.

Just when she was about to scream at him to give her a wallbanger already, he shifted lower, first with his fingers, stroking down her belly, and then with his lips and tongue. He pulled her shorts and panties off and she nearly cried with relief, but then he started all over again, his fingers stroking her belly and then around the curve of her hips.

"Zach, fuck me."

But that wasn't what he was about tonight. He didn't reply, merely stroked and kissed and tasted his way down her leg.

"Please," she whimpered.

She squirmed as he got to her sensitive calves and then the arch of her foot. When he started over, high on her other leg, she let out a mewl of protest. But it was no use. He kept moving down her leg, stroking, kissing, tasting. Finally he reached the arch of that foot and she let out a sigh of relief. That was short-lived.

His palm made a slow trip up the inside of her thigh before he finally touched where she ached for him. By the time his tongue joined his fingers, parting her and tasting her intimately, she was chanting his name, rocking mindlessly against his mouth. Oh, God.

"Zach!"

He slid his fingers inside her and looked up at her, his mouth still demanding, hungry, like all of him, his eyes heated, possessive. In that moment she was his. She knew it with startling clarity and it alarmed her. She closed her eyes.

His mouth shifted to kiss the inside of her thigh. "I want to see the ecstasy in your eyes. Will you give me that, Carrie?"

She met his eyes. A moment of charged silence vibrated between them. She sensed he was asking something significant, he rarely spoke unless he had something to say, something meaningful, but she couldn't comprehend it. Her body's need was far more powerful than her brain right now.

"Yes," she said softly.

He kissed her sex almost reverently, his eyes locked on hers. Her knees buckled, but his grip on her hips held her in place and his groan against her vibrated so intensely she gripped his head, holding him to her. She'd never felt anything so intimate, him holding her, her holding him to her most vulnerable place, his hot gaze burning into her. He amped her up with his lips and tongue and teeth, his gaze never leaving hers, and then she was coming on a long low scream, her body racked with pleasure.

He eased away from her and she closed her eyes, trying to catch her breath for what she knew would be a wild ride. The soft drop of his clothes, rustle of the condom, and then he was lifting her, taking her in one swift thrust. She scrambled to hang on, throwing her arms around him and locking her ankles behind his back. He grunted, giving her that moment before he took her with powerful thrusts, his mouth covering hers, his tongue delving deep. She was liquid fire, consumed by him, lost and found at the same time. And then she tensed on the sharp edge of ecstasy.

He tore his mouth from hers, gazing deep into her eyes. "Come for me. Look in my eyes and say my name." And then he was pounding into her and she held his gaze as long as she could before she lost it, coming and coming and coming, each thrust bringing a deeper wave of pleasure.

"Zach!" she cried.

Which must've been what he was waiting for because he let go, pumping into her for his release. His teeth closed around the cord of her neck, sending another shock wave through her.

Long moments passed. He was breathing hard, their bodies slick with sweat. Finally he lifted his head. "Carrie," he rasped.

"Zach," she said playfully, not willing to venture into the serious territory that his voice was hinting at.

He nipped her lower lip, a swift penance for her teasing. It was one of the things she liked about him most. His body spoke so clearly on a level she understood instinctively. How did he do that? She'd never had the back-and-forth with a guy the way she did with him.

"Are you going to put me down?" she asked.

He gave her a small smirk of a smile before lifting her up

and off him, setting her on her own two feet and lifting his palms in the air. She immediately had to grab his arm for balance, her legs shaky and weak from hanging on.

He chuckled.

"Jerk."

His gaze turned dark and dangerous. Her breath caught and then she was airborne, cradled in his strong arms as he carried her to the bedroom.

"You can't possibly do it again so soon," she told him.

"You can."

"By myself?"

"I'm gonna find out how many orgasms I can get out of you."

She shivered.

His voice dropped to the deep honey tone that made her crazy with lust. "I'm guessing twenty."

"N-no. No way."

"Now you're calling me out. Gotta prove myself."

She squeaked. It was all she could manage at the prospect. But the level of trust she had in him meant she had no reason to tell him no.

He set her down on the mattress, settling next to her, lying on his side. He gazed into her eyes for a long moment before his hand settled between her legs. She arched off the mattress, still sensitive.

"Easy," he crooned in her ear.

She moaned as he stroked her softly, building it up again. His deep voice in her ear, urging her on with the kind of filthy talk she'd never heard spoken out loud in her life. He kept surprising her. She stiffened suddenly and then arched into his hand as the climax hit, deeper than before.

"How many you got in you?" he whispered in her ear.

She couldn't speak. Lost in a haze.

At his mercy.

Again and again.

Until she went limp. Completely spent.

"Damn," he said. "Only three. I'll have to build you up for more."

"It was five. Two in the living room." She curled on her side and pulled the blanket over her.

He ripped it off.

"Hey!" she exclaimed, turning to face him. "Gimme that."

"My turn. Now you're gonna be my reverse cowgirl. You'll like it."

She moaned, not sure if she could take much more. He left for a moment, probably to clean up and get another condom, he respected her hard line about that. He respected *her*. An unexpected well of emotion had her tearing up. He returned, joining her in bed, and she reached for him, pulling him close in a tight hug, lying side by side. They had less than a week left.

After a few moments, she lifted her gaze to his. "Tell me what to do." Reverse cowgirl was one of his off-list requests.

His lips quirked to the side. "That might be my favorite thing you say." He rolled to his back. "Sit up and turn around."

She did and he lifted her up and then over him. She straddled him automatically, her back to him. "Oh, I get it!" she exclaimed and then gasped when he pulled her down fully onto him. She moaned loudly as her aching throbbing core took him at a different angle. He controlled her movements, holding her by the hips, taking her slow and deep. It was all too much, her body clenching down around him, her breath shallow, incredible pleasure, on and on and on, and then she was coming, a ragged cry wrenched from her throat.

He slapped her ass lightly. "More."

She swore and he tightened his grip on her hips, making her take more, over and over, soft cries escaping as he took her to a place of dark pulsing pleasure. Finally when she thought she couldn't take any more, completely spent, he stilled her, loosening his hold on her hips.

"Ride me, Carrie. Fast or slow as you want."

She started slow, but then it felt so good, she went faster and faster in an exhilarating ride. And then they were both climaxing, their voices rising together in ecstasy. She wanted to collapse, but Zach had a tight hold on her, holding her in place.

"Zach?"

He lifted her off him and set her on the bed. Then he turned her, lifting her again to settle her on top of him, chest to chest. His arms wrapped around her, giving her what she needed once more. It was that primal language they had. Or maybe it was just him. He seemed to know what she needed without her spelling it out. She wondered what the chances were of finding another man who spoke her language.

And then she dozed off, safe in his arms.

10

Zach was so relieved to have Carrie back in his arms, he immediately decided not to give another thought to a relationship and to just enjoy all that she freely gave him. His only concession to relationship territory was to go through with his promise from this morning to share a bed with her. He honored his promises, a point of pride for him, even though he knew he'd sleep like crap. He needed his space to sleep. Not even a relationship would've changed that fact.

Of course, that meant he'd had to exhaust them both. It was the only way he'd get any sleep. He wanted her out cold with no chance of even *trying* to cuddle him. Nothing worse than peeling off a cuddler. They always took offense.

He'd started the night with a wallbanger, made her come three more times, and then put her in her first reverse cowgirl. She took to it like a champion rider.

Now he looked down at her sleeping on top of him. He knew he'd pushed her pretty far on the exhaustion scale, but it wasn't yet midnight. She'd probably want more in a couple of hours. He'd rather they go straight through to mutual exhaustion and then sleep.

Fifteen minutes later, he woke her up. She protested, snuggling into his chest, so he just slid her off him to the mattress. She didn't like that.

She sat up, pouting and blinking at him, looking put-out and sexy as all hell. He sat up and slowly leaned in, watching her eyes close before he nipped and then sucked on her bottom lip. Her hands started roaming all over his chest. She was so easy to get going.

"C'mon." He got out of bed.

"Where're we going? I'm comfortable here."

He waited.

She grabbed the blanket, got out of bed, and wrapped it around her shoulders.

He pulled the blanket off her in a quick jerk and tossed it back on the bed.

"Hey!" she protested.

"I'll keep you warm." He wrapped an arm around her waist and walked with her to the living room.

Then they watched a movie.

He might've made her come a few times during the kissing scenes. It was a chick flick.

Finally it was nearly two a.m. and they were both back in bed, not sleeping. He was tired; she was tired. It should have been ideal. Unfortunately, after nine straight days of requesting and getting what was on her wish list, Carrie had become comfortable enough with him to make some demands *off* list.

"Spoon me," she said, curling on her side and scooting right up against his side where he lay on his back.

"You're a cover hog," he informed her.

"I am?" She rolled to her back and looked at him.

"Yeah."

"Here." She tossed the blanket over him, then pulled it until it covered him and hung over the other side of the bed.

"Now you'll be cold."

"That's why you have to spoon me." She rolled to her side, naked with no blanket at all, and pressed her back against his side.

He let out something that would've been a sigh from someone less bad boy than himself. "Babe."

She looked over her shoulder at him. "Babe?"

"I'm not a cuddler. I'm a lone wolf."

She giggled and rolled toward him, throwing an arm and leg over him and settling her head on his chest. "Then I'll cuddle you. Now you're a cuddled wolf."

He lay there, enjoying her soft curves pressed against him, knowing he was never going to get to sleep. He turned off the light on the nightstand and prepared for a long night. Maybe he could do some brainstorming for his long-neglected book.

She lifted her head. "Close your eyes."

"They're closed."

"I can see the whites of them."

"Then you should close your eyes."

She rubbed his chest. "Why aren't you a cuddler?"

"Don't know."

"You've never slept with a woman in your bed?"

"They sleep. I don't."

"What can I do to make it easier?"

He couldn't think of anything. His plan to exhaust them both hadn't worked. He was exhausted, though. No surprise he'd made so little progress with his book. Carrie was a full body and mind workout. He thought about her way too much. She was never far from his mind, stuff she said floating through his brain or her beauty in different lights. Like in the morning light her hair rumpled from him, sweetly sleepy, looking for her coffee. He was aware he was entering mushy territory but too tired to guard against it.

"Tell me about yourself," she whispered.

He tensed. "What do you want to know?"

"How did you meet up with the Campbells?"

He relaxed. "Their dad, Joe, was coach of the basketball team at the Police Athletic League. Ethan wanted me to play since I was tall."

"You didn't want to play?"

"I wasn't into sports, but Ethan was persistent. Turns out it's easy to be good at basketball when you're the closest one to the net."

"How old were you?" she asked in a sleepy voice.

"Nine."

She sighed, her breath fanning over his chest. "I always wished I was tall."

"You're perfect." He instantly regretted his sappy words. He understood he was on a time limit with her. But the more time he spent with her, the more he thought she was the most perfect ideal woman he'd ever met.

"Zach?"

"Yeah."

"Sometimes you surprise me with…sweetness."

He grunted. She wouldn't think he had much sweetness if she knew where he came from or how he'd pretended to be something he wasn't just to be with her. His chest tightened, gut churning with the shame he could never fully push down. *He's a bad seed. You can't trust him. Sneaky, a liar and a thief.*

"What was your troubled past?" she asked, startling him. It was like she'd read his mind. "Tell me your story."

"Who said I had a troubled past?"

"All of the guys close to the Campbells do." She lifted her head and ran her fingers through his hair, soothing him. "You can tell me. I won't judge."

He gave her part of it. "I was a repeat runaway from foster homes. I stole cash and food." He left out that his parents were in organized crime. He didn't like the association it put in people's minds and especially didn't want it in her mind. Carrie thought he was a bad boy with a little sweet on top and he was mostly okay with that.

"Oh, Zach." She gave him a squeeze around the middle. "That must've been scary for a little kid to be on the street. Of course you'd need to steal cash and food to survive. How old were you?"

"Started when I was six—"

"Omigod! Six!"

"I was fine. Street smart."

"You were lucky." She climbed on top of him and hugged him full body, her head on his chest, her arms and legs squeezing his sides.

He cupped her head and wrapped an arm around her waist.

She propped her hands on his chest and looked up at him. "Why did you keep running away? Were the foster homes bad?"

He pushed her soft hair out of her face. "They weren't all bad. Sometimes the other kids were worse than the care-givers. Tough, violent, cruel." She dropped her head on his chest and hugged him tight again. "Anyway, I ran away to find my real mom. By the time I met Joe Campbell, I was nine. He looked into it for me, found out she was dead and helped me settle into my last foster home. His house was like a second home. I spent most of my time there."

She held onto him in the longest hug of his life, probably trying to comfort him.

"Carrie, I'm fine now. Really. Joe turned things around for me." She kept right on hugging him. "Tell me your troubled past," he said to lighten the mood. He knew she'd had a good life so far. It was written all over her expressive face. She was open and enthusiastic, not beaten down by life.

She shifted to his side, one arm and leg over him and then reached up to adjust his arm around her shoulders. Bit of a forced cuddler, but he didn't mind as much as he thought he would. "My biggest heartache was wasting time on my ex, but I guess that pales in comparison to what you went through. I had a very normal middle-class childhood. My mom was a nurse, my dad a pilot, my older brother was already in college when I was born. I was a surprise baby, but even that wasn't bad. They all doted on me."

He kissed her hair. "I could tell."

"Why? Do I seem spoiled?"

"No. You just seem like someone who knows they're loved, who knows where she comes from, and has the confidence to take a few chances."

"Like with you," she said with a laugh. "Taking a chance showing my wish list to a bad boy."

He clenched his jaw. It wouldn't be long before she moved on. He'd been lucky to have her as long as he had. Lucky to have her at all, really. It made him question why he'd been working so hard these past years when the best things in his life hadn't been any work at all, just random dumb luck. Meeting her, meeting Ethan, meeting the Campbells. It suddenly occurred to him the best things in his life weren't the things he thought made him important, rising above his past—his teaching job, academic accomplishments, or even his research. It was the people he'd met. And he'd made very little time in his life for them. It all went back to his lone-wolf nature, he supposed. Kinda sucked for him and the people around him, Carrie included. It was good she wouldn't be around long enough to get hurt.

Though he hadn't actually been alone much recently, now that he thought about it. He'd been with several communities in Indonesia and a solid year with his ex, Muriel, and her family. Well, look how well *that* relationship had turned out.

Carrie interrupted his depressing thoughts. "You realize this is the longest conversation we've ever had?"

"Yeah."

"We should talk more," she said with a yawn.

"You're tired. Go to sleep," he said gruffly.

"Are you going to sleep?" she asked.

He didn't reply. The truth was he couldn't, but he didn't want to make her feel bad.

"I'll go home."

"No. Stay." He tightened his hold on her, keeping her in place against his side. He'd be damned if he was going to kick her out of bed just because he couldn't sleep. Besides, he'd made a promise. They'd sleep in the same bed, even if only one of them got a good night's sleep.

"Mmm," she said and relaxed against him.

A few minutes later, she fell asleep. He could tell because her breathing was deep and even and her entire body went limp. He waited another half hour, hoping it was long enough for her to shift into a deep state of sleep before sliding her to her side of the bed. He covered both of them with the blanket, shifted to the far edge away from her, leaving lots of space between them, and closed his eyes.

He woke surprised he'd slept past nine and in his own bed. The cover was only half on him. He turned to see Carrie wrapped with the blanket under her like a burrito on the far edge of the other side of the bed. His and hers blankets might solve the problem.

That was when he knew he had a bigger problem. Planning for a future with Carrie in it.

11

———————

Carrie had spent every night with Zach for the past twelve nights, keenly aware they were reaching the agreed upon two-week mark. Of course, that also meant she couldn't waste a single night, which was why she dragged him along with her friends to an international beer fest at Garner's on Thursday night. The event was the manager Josh's idea to push more of the high-end beer and wouldn't normally be the kind of thing her friends would attend, being more wine drinkers, but Hailey had decided it was the perfect time to finally put the rumor that Ethan was a sex addict to rest once and for all by showing everyone that she and Ethan were now a couple. This would be news to Ethan. Ha! In Hailey's mind, putting Ethan with a classy lady like herself would instantly grant him high marks. Carrie had no idea how long Hailey would pretend they were together, but figured Hailey knew what she was doing. She was the queen of happy endings with her thriving wedding planning business. In any case, it should be a very interesting evening.

Of course, this didn't qualify as a date for her and Zach. More of a two-birds-with-one-event kind of thing. That it was the second time she'd brought him along to hang with her friends was merely a matter of logistics—time crunch plus her own raging libido. She stifled a sigh. Okay, yes, she missed him fiercely when they were apart.

She glanced over at him in the driver's seat on the way to Garner's, looking all hot and sexy and alpha with his wild hair and beard, those wide shoulders, his big hand confidently steering. A traitorous warmth stole through her.

He'd gotten into her heart.

Dammit. She *knew* the moment she learned more about him, she'd start getting attached. She wished she could be less sensitive, harden herself for what was bound to be a painful separation with the two of them on opposite sides of the world. Her only defense was ending things after her parents' renewal ceremony. She knew prolonging things would only lead to a broken heart. Hers. Zach seemed tougher than that, a global traveler used to connecting with new people all the time. She was fairly certain that even though he might think back on their time fondly, he'd quickly recover. Things wouldn't be as easy for her if she let herself get in any deeper.

Zach looked over at her. "What did you tell your friends about me?"

"Why?" she hedged.

"It's the second time I'm meeting them and I'm wondering what they think I am to you. Did you tell them about the list?"

"Yes."

He shot her a quick look. "Anything else?"

"I just said you made me happy. Don't worry, I don't kiss and tell."

His lips curled in a small smile. He said nothing more, but she felt sort of giddy about that smile. He was normally so quiet and reserved that a smile was like a gift.

"If you want to hang with your friends tonight, I don't mind," Carrie said. "I just thought it would save time if we went together; then we could leave together and get back to business."

He chuckled. "We have a lot of business meetings."

"Such professionals!"

He reached over and squeezed her leg. "I came here for you, not my friends. I've been seeing them plenty."

"Oh, okay. I should warn you Hailey doesn't approve of our arrangement. It's only a matter of time before she says something. She thinks I should get to know you and give you a chance for a happy ending."

He didn't reply.

"She's a wedding planner. She can't help herself."

Another long silence.

She cleared her throat, dearly wishing she'd never brought it up. "She did make a good point about how it might be difficult, for me, anyway, to say goodbye after two weeks because I'm, you know, not used to this kind of thing."

"Uh-huh."

He said nothing more, which irritated her. Was it really just her that gave a crap about the fact that they only had three more nights and one family event left? Never mind that the time limit was her idea. Eyes hot, throat tight, she stared straight ahead. Every moment felt precious and fleeting and bittersweet.

She swallowed hard. "That's it? Just uh-huh?"

He was quiet, pulling into the parking lot behind Garner's. Finally he turned off the truck and turned to her. "What we do is between us. Not Hailey or anyone else."

"Are you used to this kind of fling thing?" She hated how her voice sounded—choked and small.

He cradled her jaw, stroking her cheek with his thumb. "No."

She took in a shaky breath. "So it might be hard for both of us to say bye after two weeks."

He closed the distance, his mouth taking hers in a long drugging kiss. It was still light out—anyone could see them making out in his truck—and that excited her. Edward had been strictly lights out and only in the bedroom. She ran her fingers through Zach's thick hair, loving the feel of the shaggy mane. She could never get enough of his kisses and never pulled away first. The kiss went on and on until she had to get closer. She undid her seatbelt, hitched up her dress, and attempted to climb into his lap.

He broke the kiss, his hands on her waist, putting her back on her side of the cab. "Mind if we're late?"

"You want to ravish me, don't you?" she asked eagerly.

He reached across her, his knuckles purposely brushing across her nipples as he reached for the seatbelt, and then skimming her nipples again as he pulled the belt back in place. He was such a wicked bad boy.

He gazed at her pointy nipples before meeting her eyes. "I want you on a blanket in the bed of my truck, spreading your legs for me."

She squirmed, already hot and wet. "I love when you talk dirty."

He held her chin. "I love when you *are* dirty."

She laughed, giddy again. "Yes, let's go."

They made love under the setting sun by a lake Zach knew about deep in a nature preserve. She was extremely comfortable first on a thick sleeping bag he'd set out for her and then on top of him. He made a wonderfully warm mattress.

After, she rested her head on his chest, listening to his heart pounding. "Zach?"

"Mmm."

"What're we doing?" She lifted her head and waited for him to open his eyes. "Are we being stupid putting a time limit on things?"

His voice was rough and gravelly. "You tell me."

"I don't know."

He slid his fingers through her hair, cradling her head. "Here's what I do know, you had a specific goal, try out a few items. I had a specific goal, be the one to make that happen and keep you safe. If we keep this thing going, that's deeper territory. And we both know we're heading in different directions soon. Literally."

She blinked, a little stunned not only at the flood of words from a man of so few words, but also that he got to the heart of the matter so succinctly. He was right, of course. She started grad school here in a little over a week; he was heading to Singapore soon. Besides, he'd said he didn't do long-term. She shivered, suddenly cold despite his heat under her. His arms closed around her, pulling her tight against him, warming her. She told herself to get off him, but she couldn't seem to move, every part of her needing this closeness. His heartbeat under her ear steadied her. It would be way too easy to let herself fall. Way too difficult to recover. And she refused to give up on her own dream of graduate school just to be with him.

She lifted her head and stared into the face of the man she had to learn to let go. He studied her in his quiet observant way, running his fingers through her hair. It didn't make sense to push him to give long-term a try when they wouldn't even be on the same continent. And was she really ready for another relationship, or was it just post-sex bliss that made her imagine a different future for them? How could anyone think clearly lying naked in their lover's arms? It swayed her thinking and she needed to stay sharp.

She smiled. "You have a keen analytical mind, don't you?"

One side of his mouth quirked up in a bemused expression.

"How come you didn't take me here for a Sunday drive the first time? Ethan probably wouldn't have found us here."

"Yeah, he could've if he wasn't working. He comes here all the time fishing and camping. Anyway, it's much harder to get in and out of this place in the dark. No streetlights."

She kissed him. "Let's go. Poor Ethan has no idea why Hailey has decided to make him hers."

He sat up, bringing her with him, one arm around her waist. "He knows. I told him yesterday. He says he likes flirting with Hailey, but now that he knows her ulterior motive is to kill that ridiculous rumor, he's out. He's bringing backup to put the rumor to rest *his* way."

Her jaw dropped. "Omigod! You told him? You weren't supposed to tell him." *And won't Hailey be surprised?*

He watched her with hooded eyes. "I don't always do what I'm supposed to do."

Such a rebel. She lifted off him, reached for her bra and pulled it on.

He stroked a hand down her side and over her hip. She loved that he still wanted to touch her after sex. There was something almost reverent about his touch afterward that made her want to purr and rub against him like a contented cat. Or maybe she was just reading into things, imagining a tenderness in him that wasn't there. Maybe he was touching her and thinking about having her again. They did have a lot of sex. She really had no idea what was in his head. Maybe nothing at all. She went cold all over and grabbed her dark green dress, quickly pulling it on.

"Help!" Her arm was stuck. Zach helped her straighten out the twisted cap sleeve and get the dress on. She leaned back and slipped on her panties. "Meet you back in front."

She stood up and he gave her a light slap on the ass. "Zach!"

"Can't help it. You've got the prettiest ass I've ever seen."

She smiled to herself and got out of the bed of the truck, hopping down and slipping on her heels. Sometimes he said the sweetest things.

He joined her a few minutes later and they drove over to Garner's in comfortable silence, the edge of hard lust temporarily satisfied between them. She'd craved passion with every cell in her being and found it with Zach. She liked to think it was his skill and her enthusiasm that made the incredible heat between them because that meant she could find it again. The alternative was unbearable to think about.

She quickly decided she definitely wasn't ready to jump into another relationship. Getting over Edward had been like going through a divorce after six long years, especially because they'd started when she was only nineteen. He was the blueprint for all future relationships, her only experience. It had been good with Edward in the beginning; he'd gone all out with a steady stream of flowers, candy, jewelry, dinner by candlelight, the works. Now she realized things between them had worked mostly because she was so young and inexperienced, eager to please him and willing to conform to his expectations. He'd been seven years older, just out of medical school and seemed so sophisticated. As she got started in her own career, taking responsibility for patients, she'd changed, standing up for what she wanted. He'd been less than pleased.

Zach held the door to Garner's open for her and she stepped inside to quite a crowd. They headed straight for the bar, waiting their turn for a drink. She looked around for Ethan and his "backup." Oh, wow, interesting. Ethan was sitting in a booth in the dining area. Next to him was a tough-looking woman with a short dark cap of hair, sharp cheekbones, and a black tank top that showed off the sculpted muscles of her arms. Across from them sat Hailey, who appeared to be leading the conversation while Ethan and the other woman occasionally responded in between devouring a pile of chicken wings.

Josh appeared in front of Zach and offered an international beer sampler with five small glasses of beer. Zach took him up on it. Before Carrie could try one, Ally grabbed her arm and pulled her farther away by their friends.

Ally grinned. "So, things going well with Zach, huh? Now you're actually showing up places with him like a real boyfriend not just a fuck buddy."

"Shh."

"Nothing wrong with a fuck buddy," Missy put in from Ally's other side.

"It's still a short-term thing," Carrie confided. She quickly changed the subject, asking Ally about her preparations for the new school year (she was a first-grade teacher), and then catching up on what was new with everyone. She made herself focus on her friends, but finally the temptation to seek out Zach proved too much and she peeked over at him. He sat on a bar stool, holding a beer and listening to some of the guys. Even laid-back Josh was leaning across the bar, talking and joking around with the guys. It struck her that Zach, even in the middle of a group of guys he knew well, seemed separate. The observer. What was going on in his head? She wondered if he had nothing to say or if he had tons of thoughts bouncing around in there that he never let out. And then she wondered if she'd ever find out. She caught Zach's eye and the chatter of her friends, the clinking of glasses, even the sound of the TV above the bar receded far in the distance. Every part of her wanted to reach out to him in that moment and be let *in*.

He stood, seeming to read her thoughts from across the room, and crossed to her, slipping an arm around her waist from behind. For some reason, she was blushing, though she should be well used to his touch after nearly two weeks of naked time. He never hesitated to hook an arm around her and pull her close. Even late at night in bed, now that they both slept in the bed, the last thing he did was hook an arm around her shoulders and tuck her tight against his side. Somehow she always woke up on the far edge of the bed away from him.

"You remember everyone?" she asked Zach.

"Yeah. Hi," Zach said.

"Hello," her friends chorused.

"Of course we remember you!" Ally exclaimed. "You're *the man*."

Carrie glanced back at Zach to see if he was embarrassed hearing what Carrie had called him right before she'd seduced him that first night they met, but he took it in stride. "Yup." He spoke in a low rumble by her ear, giving her a shiver. "You want something to drink? I know you're not a big beer drinker."

"I'll take a piña colada," she said.

He released her waist, his hand grazing across her back as he shifted down to the other end of the bar to put in the order with Josh. She was just listening to Ally, who was counting down the days until her college reunion, where she hoped to get back together with her ex, when Zach returned with a bar stool. He asked one of the guys to shift down and set it next to Ally's stool before pulling Carrie up and onto his lap, his arm banding around her waist, keeping her securely in place.

Ally kept right on talking, but she also took in the casual gesture with interest. Carrie rested her hand on Zach's arm and tried to focus on the conversation. An impossibility. She was hyperaware of him, skin hot, every nerve ending stirring to life, aching for his touch, his spicy sexy scent making her nearly light-headed with need.

Josh appeared a few minutes later, setting her drink with a cute little umbrella in it in front of her.

"Thanks!" she said.

"You got it," Josh said. He turned to Zach. "How's your book coming along?"

"No book," Zach muttered.

Carrie tilted her head back to look at Zach, who was staring at Josh. "What book?" she asked.

Zach shifted his hand, splaying his fingers low on her belly in a gesture her body recognized as a precursor to seduction. It was an under-the-bar move, but she felt herself flush anyway. She took a sip of piña colada, trying to act as if everything was normal despite the low ache in her womb and the dampness between her legs.

Josh shifted his gaze to Carrie, giving her a wink and a charming smile. "We started our own book club just for us men."

"You did?" she asked, surprised.

"That's right," Josh said, leaning close to share in a confidential manner. "We're reading *What Women Want*."

Her eyes widened and she checked in with Zach, looking back at him. His expression gave nothing away.

Josh's brown eyes danced with good humor. "Except Zach here refuses to read the book. Says he knows it all. What do you think, Carrie? Is he right?"

"Depends what the book says," she said with a grin. "Do tell."

"Yeah, I want to hear this too," Ally chimed in.

"Bah. I didn't read it either," Josh said, meeting Zach's eyes for a moment before shifting to the dining area. "It was all Ethan's idea. Poor guy lacks experience. Someone should warn Hailey off."

"Eth's got two women interested in him," Zach said casually. "Looks like he'll get experience real soon."

Josh narrowed his eyes at Zach. Carrie glanced back to find Zach grinning. Okay, then. She bit back a smile.

Ally changed the subject, probably trying to hold off another Josh-Hailey smackdown. Their frenemy thing had gotten a little out of hand lately. They were a little sharper and snippier than just a casual joking/flirting/bantering back and forth. Her friend Lauren, a natural peacemaker, had tried to smooth things over between the pair, encouraging them each to be the bigger person and outsweet each other, with *zero* results.

Hailey strode over, standing next to Ally, and announced for the benefit of everyone in the bar, "Welp, Ethan has a new girlfriend, Cali Boggs. She's pretty kick-ass and it seems serious." She flipped her strawberry blond hair over one shoulder. "Super classy too," she added before saying in a lower confidential tone, "Good thing I realized Ethan and I had zero chemistry. We're so much better off as friends." She didn't sound upset in the least. In fact, she sounded cheerfully relieved, probably because everything had worked out. Now Ethan was clearly not a sex addict, with a classy girlfriend, and Hailey could go back to what she liked best—helping other people find love. Carrie suspected Hailey had never experienced love herself, but she never wanted to make Hailey feel bad about that, so she kept her mouth shut.

Hailey turned and took in Carrie sitting in Zach's lap. "Hello. You two look happy."

"We are," Carrie said, hoping to avoid any further embarrassing questions.

Zach made a noise that might have been a grunt of agreement, his hand still sprawled low on her belly, the heat and intent revving her up. He knew what he was doing to her since she freely shared how he made her feel physically. She couldn't help herself. Passion was still such a new thrilling experience that she just blurted everything in her excitement.

Josh smirked at Hailey. "Looks like you're running out of people to set up, princess."

Hailey lifted her chin. "What about you?"

Josh shifted, suddenly uncomfortable. "What about me?"

"In my professional opinion—" Hailey paused dramatically "—you're a die-hard bachelor in need of a woman to soften your harsh."

Josh crossed his arms, making his biceps bulge. "I'm not harsh. I'm charming."

"Ha!" Hailey returned. "Ha-ha-ha! That must be why you're always alone."

Carrie sucked in a breath. All of their friends went quiet.

Mad, Josh's sister, piped up from a few seats away. "Harsh."

Hailey bit her lip. "Josh, I—"

"You don't know everything," Josh returned easily, letting her off the hook. "I pick up women all the time." He gestured Hailey over to the guys sitting at the other end of the bar. "Move along, princess, because I don't see you with anyone either. Let's see your pickup moves. If you have any. Looks like you crashed and burned with Eth."

Carrie glanced over to see Hailey making an unusually snarly face at Josh, who pulled his phone from his pocket and snapped a picture. "That face is going online."

"What do you mean?" Hailey asked.

"Facebook, Insta, the works," Josh replied, tapping a few keys and smirking.

Hailey leaped forward, grabbing for the phone across the bar. "Gimme that, you beast!" She always called him old-fashioned names—scoundrel, cad, and beast being the top three—straight from the old-timey romantic comedy movies she loved. Josh called her one thing—princess.

Josh leaned back, out of reach, and held up the phone again, aiming it at her. "Keep it up. Let's see your pissed-off princess face."

Hailey growled. Josh snapped another picture and showed it to her.

"I swear I will—" Hailey shut up quickly when Josh held up his phone again.

"Video too," he said with a smirk. "Keep it up."

Hailey seethed, her cheeks flushed bright pink. She pulled

her phone from her purse and tapped a few buttons. Probably checking for notifications.

Zach whispered in Carrie's ear, "Josh doesn't do social media. He stays off the radar."

Carrie immediately slipped her phone out of her purse and texted Hailey, letting her know. Girl code.

Hailey's demeanor completely changed as she read the text, from pissed off back to composed. She shot Carrie a grateful look, tucked her phone away, and stood next to Carrie, facing her nemesis across the bar. "Josh, our squabbling has become tiresome. I don't want a showdown every time I come in here."

Josh tucked his phone in his back jeans pocket, his dark eyes lit with anticipation. "Yeah?"

Hailey smiled her pasted-on beauty-queen smile. It popped up in high-stress situations. "I think we should go back to the beginning. Right the wrong so we can move forward."

Josh arched a brow.

Hailey tossed her hair. "You owe me five hundred large."

Josh stepped closer. "You realize large means a thousand, right? I owe you five *hundred*. That's it." That was the grand total Hailey had previously paid Josh to be her escort at the many weddings she planned. Their arrangement had ended suddenly with the typical flare-up of tempers between them.

Hailey lifted her chin, looked around to their friends, who were all watching and silently supporting her. Carrie gave her an encouraging smile. Hailey turned back to Josh. "Well, it's large to me."

Josh snickered.

Hailey soldiered on. "I would like that money returned so we're on even footing."

Josh inclined his head. "Come and get it."

Hailey bristled. "No, you can give it to me."

"Here we go!" Mad chortled. The women shushed her. This was where things fell apart last time. Josh had the money at his apartment. Hailey refused to go there.

Josh grinned devilishly. "I told ya it's back at my place. All ya gotta do is—" his voice dropped low and taunting "—come and get it."

Hailey put her hands on her hips and retorted, "I'm not setting foot in that den of sin!"

Josh threw back his head and laughed. Carrie had to wonder what exactly a den of sin looked like. Whips and chains? Stripper poles? Red velvet walls?

"So you won't bring it here?" Hailey asked.

"Nope," Josh replied.

"Then I would like an escort." She looked around to some of the men, her gaze landing on Zach.

"Don't put me in the middle of this," Zach said.

It didn't matter. Josh was already stepping out from behind the bar, heading straight for Hailey. He stopped next to her and crooked his elbow, offering his arm in a gentlemanly way. The Campbell men were all very good with the gentleman manners.

"Not you!" Hailey said, glaring at his offered arm.

"Why not?" Josh asked. "I've escorted you before."

Carrie turned to Zach. "He means down the aisle."

"Not at our wedding!" Hailey exclaimed. "We're not married. We're not anything."

Josh let out a breath of clear exasperation. "What's it gonna be, princess?"

Hailey scowled. "Go away."

"Chicken."

"Don't talk to me ever again. I mean it."

"Never?" Josh teased. "What if there's a fire?"

Hailey pursed her lips. "Then tell someone else."

"Tornado?" Mad put in, earning a dark look from Hailey.

"Unlikely," Hailey returned.

Josh grinned. "Earthquake?"

Hailey lifted her palms. "When was the last time Connecticut had an earthquake?"

Carrie felt Zach chuckle under her. They were pretty funny. She was glad they'd gone back to their usual banter. She'd been a little worried there about hurt feelings.

Josh kept going, looking thoroughly entertained. "Tsunami?"

Hailey crossed her arms. "Now you're being ridiculous. We're too far inland for that."

Josh gave her hair a tug. "I'll get you your favorite drink." He walked back behind the bar while Hailey morphed from surprised to extraordinarily pleased.

Ally got up from her bar stool. "Here, Hailey, take my seat and enjoy your drink. You've more than earned it."

"Thanks so much!" Hailey exclaimed. "I really appreciate it." She took the offered seat and watched as Josh prepared her favorite drink, a mojito.

He served it up with a flourish. "Bottoms up, princess."

Hailey grabbed the glass and paused, taking a moment to announce to anyone who happened to be listening, which was all of them, that she and Josh were officially at peace. She lifted the glass to her lips and then added with a small smirk, "No more fighting because we're no longer speaking."

"Even during emergency weather situations," Josh quipped.

Everyone laughed.

Hailey finished taking a long drink before lifting a finger to her lips in a gesture of shushing at Josh.

"Ri-i-i-ght," Josh said. "Not speaking." Then he gave her a big wink.

The women tittered. This was a callback to when Hailey had announced he wasn't impotent and then gave a big wink to indicate she was joking (which, of course, had the effect of sounding like he actually *was* impotent). These two. Really. Out of control.

Hailey let out a long dramatic sigh. "Okay. You may speak to me in emergency situations." She took another sip of mojito and let out a happy sigh.

Josh snapped a picture with his phone. "Mojito orgasm face. That's definitely going online."

"Go for it," Hailey said and took another blissful sip of her long-denied drink.

Josh put his phone away and scanned the group. "Aw, come on. Who's the rat?"

Zach spoke up, taking the fall for Carrie. He must've figured out Carrie's texting was spilling the beans to Hailey that Josh didn't actually do social media. "Hailey probably noticed you didn't have a Facebook account or whatever. Nice subterfuge, though."

"Subterfuge," Josh muttered, scowling at Zach. "Big word. Thanks a lot, Professor."

Carrie looked back at Zach. "Professor?"

Zach just shook his head and then whispered in her ear, "Let's get out of here. I've got plans for you." He set her back on her feet and rested his hand on the small of her back like he often did when they walked together. He waited, probably to see if she was on board. She was more than ready. Her libido was tuned in to his frequency and she wouldn't refuse him anything. Except her heart.

"Bye!" she told her friends.

"Have fun!" Ally hollered.

"Bring him by next Thursday after book club!" Hailey called.

Carrie just waved, some part of her sinking at the cheerful sentiment, knowing that next Thursday was never going to happen. But she had tonight and she fully intended to make the most of it.

"Why did Josh call you professor?" she asked Zach once they were outside.

"Because I'm smart. Just like he calls Hailey princess because she's beautiful."

"That's why he calls her princess? I thought he was saying she was snooty."

"It always comes back to biology," he said matter-of-factly.

That struck her as an odd way to look at it. But before she could comment on that, he leaned down and kissed her. All thoughts flew from her mind once her body got the message it was time for her bad boy. Maybe everything did come back to biology.

12

Carrie was a nervous wreck. She had to pull herself together before her parents' vow renewal ceremony. She was only partially ready, had to leave in twenty minutes, and couldn't make any decisions. "Ally! Help!" she hollered from her bedroom.

Ally burst in, eyes wide. "What's wrong?"

"Which earrings look better?" She had one silver hoop and one pearl earring in.

Ally walked over and flicked her on the arm.

"Ow!" She rubbed her arm.

"Don't scream help unless it's an emergency. You ever hear of the boy who cried wolf?"

"Look at me." She held up her shaking hands. "I'm falling apart."

"Geez, sit down." Ally grabbed her by the wrist and dragged her to sit on the bed. "You look smoking hot in that dress."

Carrie glanced down at the white off-the-shoulder dress that cinched in at the waist. It was new. Somehow she couldn't muster any enthusiasm for her outfit. "Thanks," she mumbled.

"Hey, you're going to be fine," Ally said firmly. "Just be

polite to Edward and then ignore him. You've both moved on."

Carrie crossed her arms, hugging herself. "It's not just that. Well, it is, but now I'm thinking I made a big mistake inviting Zach. My parents are going to meet him. They're going to ask about him later and wonder why he's not around anymore."

"Are you definitely not seeing him after this?"

"Yes. He found out he got the job in Singapore. He leaves right after Christmas for two years. That's halfway around the world! Besides, this was only supposed to be a short-term thing. He even said he doesn't do long-term." She pressed a hand to her churning stomach. "I feel a little sick just talking about it."

"So what's wrong with seeing each other for a few months before he leaves?"

"It'll just make the goodbye harder. Anyway, it's not a real relationship. Just a lot of sex. We barely speak to each other." Well, that wasn't exactly true anymore. Now that they slept in the same bed, they talked before they fell asleep. And at breakfast too.

Was this a relationship?

No. It felt too easy. They were just having some fun together. It wasn't like they talked about anything that deep. Zach had been telling her about Indonesia, sounding very much like the tour guide he was.

She could feel herself getting worked up again about seeing her ex. "There's so many opportunities for this to go wrong! What if Edward's a jerk to Zach? What if Zach gets mad and tells him off?"

Ally rubbed Carrie's arm. "That wouldn't be so bad. He'd be defending your honor. Like a knight in shining armor."

"This is *not* a fairy tale."

Ally spoke gently. "I'm sure no one is going to make a scene at such a special occasion. Just think of your parents' happiness. Be there for them."

She immediately felt calmer. It was in her nature to take care of other people. That was what made nursing such a good fit for her. "Thanks for the pep talk. You're right. Today isn't about me."

Ally stood. "Tell your parents congratulations for me. Now hurry up and get ready." She left.

Carrie headed for the bathroom, taking extra care with her hair and makeup. She felt so petty, but she had to show Edward that she'd moved on and was doing fine. Look what you missed out on! Who cares that you're about to marry someone younger and more beautiful than me? Not that she'd seen the woman, but the way her mom had sounded so sympathetic when she'd told Carrie about her, she was sure she was gorgeous. Who cares? Their sex life probably sucked.

A short while later, the doorbell rang. Ally got to it first. "Omigod! You look so different! Carrie, Zach's here!"

She rushed to the living room. "Hi! Omigod is right!"

Zach ducked his head, smiling almost shyly. "I told ya I'd clean up."

She approached slowly, her heart thumping hard at the shocking transformation. He'd gotten a haircut, short with some spiky layers on top, his beard and mustache short in a neat trim, his tall lean frame in a dark gray suit with a crisp white shirt and gray tie. It wasn't that he looked *bad*. He looked very handsome. Just nothing like the alpha bad boy she knew.

He leaned down to her ear, his hand cupping her shoulder. "You look beautiful."

"You too! I just can't believe the difference! Let me see the back."

He turned and she ran her fingers through the short fine hair at the nape of his neck. No more thick hair to sink her fingers into, no more wave.

She sighed, mourning the loss.

He turned and tipped her chin up. "It'll grow back."

"You look like a lawyer or something," she blurted.

His lips crooked to the side. "I'm not. Ready?"

She nodded.

He turned to Ally. "Nice to see you again."

Ally beamed. "Have fun!"

She walked out the door with Zach, his hand resting on the small of her back as he led her to his truck. He even opened the passenger-side door and helped her get in so she wouldn't mess up her nice white dress. She looked down at him all clean-cut and good manners in a suit he could wear to church. "My parents are going to love you," she said forlornly.

His lips twitched. "Would you rather they didn't?"

"They're going to ask about you later. They'll want to have you over for dinner."

He gazed into her eyes. "I'd be happy to go."

"You would?"

He dipped his head and went around to the driver's side.

She smoothed her dress, her hands suddenly clammy.

Zach got in and pulled out of the lot.

"You know how to get there?" she asked.

"Yeah."

He had grown up around here. She stared out the window, taking a deep breath as the panicky feeling returned. She didn't know if it was Zach or Edward that was getting her worked up, she only knew she had to pull herself together fast. What was Zach thinking saying he'd have dinner with her parents? They'd both been very clear about this being their last night together. It was. It had to be. No matter how many unexpectedly sweet things Zach said, she had to hold firm to that for her own good. She tucked her trembling hands under her legs.

Zach reached over and squeezed her leg. "You'll do great. I got your back."

"Thanks," she murmured. "I'm sure the anticipation is worse than the actual event. Right?"

"Usually."

That didn't make her feel any better. Not much could, it seemed.

"Tell me about your family," he said.

"My dad, Mark, says it was love at first sight when he met my mom, Judy." She launched into the favorite family story of how they met when her mom was her dad's nurse for a physical. "She made my heart skip a beat!" Carrie said in a deep impersonation of her dad's jovial voice.

Zach chuckled.

She kept going, sharing the way her dad had pursued her mom with bouquets of flowers, each one accompanied by a terribly rhyming poem about her beauty. Then she told him about her big brother, Rich, now a pilot like her dad was before he retired. She'd become a nurse just like her mom. She figured it all sounded kind of boring, but just talking about her family calmed her nerves.

Before she knew it, they were pulling into the parking lot. She could see the wedding pavilion in the distance with a small brick patio where the chairs were set up. On the opposite side stood a white tent for the reception. She stepped out of the truck and admired the Long Island Sound beyond the pavilion with its softly lapping waves. It was always a bit cooler by the Sound and felt wonderful. The ceremony would be in an hour, close to sunset. They'd arrived early so she could help with any last minute setup stuff her parents might need.

They ran into her brother, Rich, first, who gave her a brief hug. He was tall, but not as tall as Zach, his dirty blond hair in a crew cut, clean-shaven, and had sharp blue eyes. She quickly introduced him to Zach.

"Nice to meet you," Rich said, grabbing Zach's hand in a firm manly handshake and holding his gaze directly.

"You too," Zach said, his expression just as serious as her brother's.

She could almost feel the testosterone spike as they sized each other up. Zach must've passed because her brother immediately put Zach to work, helping him haul additional chairs in place under the tent.

Carrie met up with her nieces and sister-in-law and helped them add white streamers and bows to the chairs by the wedding pavilion as well as arrange some flowers for a beautiful backdrop. When she finished, she found Zach waiting for her at the end of the aisle. She had to fight the impulse to run down the aisle and leap into his arms. It was what she did after every separation. That moment of connection was like bottled sunshine bursting through her in radiant joy. If only all of their moments could be that simple.

He held his arms out to her like he knew what she wanted to do. She laughed and shook her head, instead walking sedately over to him. He hooked her around the waist and pulled her close.

She smiled up at him. "How'd it go with my brother?"

He inclined his head, a small smile playing over his lips. "He invited me to have cigars after the ceremony, but I don't smoke."

"He shouldn't be either! Geez, he's still smoking cigars! Gross. As a nurse, I'm offended."

Zach stroked her back. "The point is more symbolic. The gesture invites familiarity and acceptance."

Her jaw dropped. "Are you a shrink?"

"No."

"Who's not a shrink?" a familiar masculine voice said from behind her. Carrie turned and gave her dad a hug and a kiss on the cheek. He was seventy-two, but with the energy of a much younger man. Her mom was seventy with matching vitality.

"How're you, sweetheart?" her dad asked, glancing at Zach curiously, who stood next to her, looking solid and respectable.

"I'm good, Dad. Love the tux." She adjusted the lapels of his white tux. His white hair matched, neatly parted to the side. "You're a handsome groom."

"Thank you," her dad said. "And who's this young man?"

Zach offered his hand. "Zach Harrison, nice to meet you, Mr. Young."

"You too. Call me Mark." Her dad shook his hand and turned to Carrie. "You been dating long? Your mom hasn't mentioned you were seeing anyone." His brows drew together and she knew he was a little hurt to be left out of her life.

"No, not long," she assured him. "Just a couple weeks."

Her dad turned to Zach. "Where're your people from?"

"Dad!"

"What?" her dad exclaimed. "I'm just making conversation."

Zach straightened to his full height, shoulders back, chin up. He reminded her of a soldier, which was so at odds with his usual easy grace, she felt herself getting worked up in sympathy for him having to undergo the protective-father third degree.

"I grew up in Connecticut," Zach said and offered nothing more.

"Mmm," her dad said, rolling back and forth on the balls of his feet. "And where did you go to school?"

Carrie clenched her teeth. Really, all of this awkward talk was completely unnecessary.

"Well, sir," Zach started with a quick glance to her.

"You don't have to answer all his questions," Carrie put in. "Dad, please."

"Mark?" her mom called.

Her dad jumped and then clapped once. "Oh! I'd better go check on my lovely bride." He took off to the side of the brick patio behind a trellis covered in greenery and white flowers. It was where the bridal party would wait for the big moment.

"Isn't it bad luck to see the bride before the ceremony?" Zach asked.

"Maybe I should go see if I can help." She hurried over there. "You guys need any—ah!" She slapped a hand over her eyes. Her parents were making out.

"Carrie! So good to see you, honey!" her mom exclaimed.

Carrie dropped her hand. Her mom looked stunning, her white blond hair arranged in soft waves to her shoulders, her skin glowing. She wore a simple empire-waist white wedding gown with a long veil perched on her head, trailing behind her. "Hi, Mom, sorry to intrude."

Her mom gave her a big hug. "No worries. I can't wait to meet Zach."

Carrie glanced at her dad, who was grinning mischievously. "Isn't it bad luck to see the bride beforehand?"

Her dad wrapped his arm around her mom's waist. "We

had to recreate the frantic kissing moment before our first wedding. Your mom couldn't keep her hot little hands off me!"

"Oh, Mark!" Her mom giggled. "I'm sure that was more you than me."

Her dad leered at her mom and then turned to Carrie. "I know it's a little superstitious, but hey! It's worked for fifty years, don't want to break the tradition. Can you give us a minute?" He pulled her mom in close.

Carrie rushed out of there.

She found Zach standing on the beach just steps from the white tent, looking out to the water. "They were making out behind the trellis," she informed him.

His brows shot up. "Lucky."

"What do you mean?"

"I mean fifty years of marriage and they can't keep their hands off each other is damn lucky."

She'd never thought about it that way. Her parents were just always there. She'd always thought it normal, boring even. They fought infrequently. They did everything together, especially now that they were both retired. Sometimes they just seemed like one person. She'd once thought the same thing would happen for her with Edward, a long and happy life together. A normal life. House in the suburbs, vacations on the lake, the kids she'd always wanted. That dream had been shattered with Edward's betrayal.

Now she wasn't sure if it'd ever happen for her. And she didn't want that anymore, anyway. The kids part she did want, she loved kids. It was just that she couldn't imagine how marriage could ever give the thrill and excitement of a fling. The kind of heat she shared with Zach must burn out eventually. Right? Wait, was that what her parents had behind closed doors? *Eww. Don't think about it.*

She crossed her arms, hugging herself. She'd never know with Zach. It was better that way. Go out on a high note. Her stomach rolled and she forced herself to focus on her parents' special day. "Let's go see what else we can do to help."

She turned and went back to the pavilion. Zach followed, sticking close to her side.

More people arrived and Carrie and her brother acted as ushers, guiding them to the bride's or groom's side. Zach sat on the end of the back row, watching every person she talked to and she knew exactly why. He was waiting to meet her ex. He wouldn't leave her alone to face him.

And then he was there. Dr. Edward Zigler standing with a petite brunette, long glossy hair, big doe-like eyes, in a beautiful peach sundress that clung to a huge baby bump. Carrie's stomach lurched. Oh, God. She felt nauseous. Edward looked the same, arrogant and proud in a dark blue custom-tailored suit. His blond hair was short, ice blue eyes, sharp cheekbones, patrician nose, full lips. He was handsome as always yet so cold.

They were heading straight for her. She sucked in air. The woman had to be eight months pregnant. Carrie and Edward had only broken up a little over a year ago. How did he move on so quickly to marriage and baby? Why didn't her mom mention the baby? Suddenly a strong arm wrapped around her shoulders and she sank gratefully against Zach's side. Zach pulled her close and kissed her temple, boosting her confidence.

Edward and the pregnant lady stopped in front of her. "Carrie," he said brusquely. Like he barely knew her after six long years. They'd lived together for three of them! And she'd fucking known him her entire fucking life!

"Hello, Edward," she said through her teeth. "It's been a long time."

Edward smiled smugly. "Yes, a lot's happened. All for the good. This is my fiancée, Tara."

"Hi," Tara said in the softest, gentlest voice Carrie had ever heard. This was what Edward wanted, a young gentle girl he could mold to fit his life. She wondered if he was still doing the kinky sex app to keep his future wife pure. Her stomach rolled. Not her problem anymore.

"Hi." She stared at the woman's pregnant belly, still in shock. That could've been *her*. Married with a kid on the way.

Instead she was merrily fucking her way through a sex list. Her life was about sex. His was about real stuff—love and home and family. It shouldn't have hurt as much as it did. But it did hurt. Terribly. Her throat was tight, her eyes stinging, her gut churning.

"I'm Zach."

She belatedly turned to find Zach staring Edward down. Zach didn't offer his hand.

"We'll go take a seat," Edward said stiffly.

"Yes, please sit on the groom's side," she said numbly.

"Let's go, honey," Edward said, guiding his young pregnant fiancée to a seat.

Carrie watched them go, trembling slightly from the encounter. Edward had proposed to her with a large diamond ring after they broke up—a too little, too late gesture. It had been the last straw in a long line of controlling manipulative moves on his part.

So why did she suddenly feel like bawling her eyes out?

What the hell was she doing with her life? With Zach?

She finished her job ushering in friends and family in a haze. Then it was time for her to walk down the aisle as her mom's maid of honor. Zach stayed in the last row and she couldn't see him very well from where she stood behind the bride. All she could see was the happy look on her dad's face as he vowed to love her mom forever for a second time.

The young pregnant woman in peach—Tara, she reminded herself—sat just beyond her dad in Carrie's direct line of vision. She clenched her jaw and willed herself to be happy for her parents and think of nothing else.

She could cry later. Alone.

13

———

Zach caught up with Carrie at the reception once she'd finished helping her parents get comfortable and serving them some food and drink. He'd never seen Carrie at work as a nurse, but he imagined she was just like this, helpful and competent no matter how she felt on the inside. He knew seeing her ex with a pregnant fiancée had thrown her. She'd paled and wavered on her feet. He'd been afraid she was about to pass out.

He sat under the white tent at a round table with Carrie's brother, sister-in-law, and two nieces. Rich and his wife were in a deep discussion over something to do with their teenage daughter, who wanted to leave early to meet up with her boyfriend. Carrie was standing next to her seat, near him, taking some video of her parents slow dancing on the dance floor, the only couple out there. Very sweet couple. He couldn't remember ever seeing a couple like that, still crazy about each other after fifty years. He wondered what their secret was, how they made it work for so long and still be so into each other. It was rare. Maybe even worthy of some study. What gave a relationship longevity? He pushed that from his mind, recognizing it was a purely selfish pursuit, trying to figure out how to break from his lone-wolf pattern and find everlasting happiness. They were exceptional. He was not.

"Carrie! Rich! Come out here too!" her mom called.

He watched as Carrie had a dance with her brother and then her dad and then she gestured to him. He stood and joined them along with Rich's wife.

He slid an arm around Carrie's back and took her hand, taking the lead.

Her hand went to his shoulder, her head tipping back to look up at him. "You can dance!"

He pulled her close, whispering in her ear, "I'm a man of many talents."

She pulled back and stared at him. "Who are you, and what have you done with my wild man?"

He chuckled, glad she was in better spirits now. "How're you doing?"

"Fine. I'm not jealous. I'm happy for them." She went up on tiptoe and whispered, "A couple glasses of champagne helped."

He knew she couldn't hold her liquor, so that small amount had probably dulled the sharp edges for her. "Do you wish it had been you, engaged and pregnant?"

"No!" she fired back with enough heat that he knew some part of her did.

He didn't know what to say to make it better, so he just danced. But he knew what to do. Treat her like a queen. He hadn't shown her the gentleman side of himself, purposely keeping it hidden, but it was a part of him. A big part. His honorary dad, Joe, had taught him in word and deed, as well as a number of hilarious lessons throughout his teen years.

He smiled to himself, remembering the first time Joe had sat them down in his living room, the four oldest of the gang —Josh, Jake, Zach, and Marcus—at the ripe age of fourteen. (Marcus was only thirteen, but already very into girls.) First they got the Talk—plain facts about sex, consent, and protection that made them squirm. Then Joe announced he was going to teach them how to treat a woman. They'd leaned in, eager to hear some sex secrets.

"Like your little sister," was the disappointing answer. "Pretend they're Mad."

"Blech!" "Gross!" "Barf!" erupted from the guys.

"Hold on," Joe said, lifting a hand. "Think how you'd want a guy to treat her, huh? Respectfully, carefully, *kindly*. Like a gentleman."

Ethan, still a punk with a big chip on his shoulder, sneered. "I'm not a frigging gentleman."

Joe stood, an imposing man, tall and fit like a cop should be. "Alright, outside, you knuckleheads."

They all got off the sofa and made their slow swaggering way to the door.

Then Joe announced, "I'm going to demonstrate lesson one—opening doors. Ethan, you'll be the girl."

Ethan halted, his cheeks flaming red. "Like hell. I'm outta here."

Joe snagged Ethan by the back of the collar. "I'll be the girl."

Everyone laughed. Manly Joe playing a girl was hilarious just to think about.

They got outside to Joe's car, where he stood by the passenger side. "Now let's practice. Ethan, you're up."

Ethan was so relieved not to be the girl that he fell in line nicely, opening and shutting the door for "the girl."

Joe always seemed to know how to reach each of them.

They'd all taken a turn, opening and closing a car door and then the house door, letting Joe go first. Not their last hands-on lesson either. The man was determined the crop of boys under his watch would treat women right. Later, Joe had shared why these lessons were important. His mom had been abused by his dad before she finally left him. Years later, Joe's stepdad had been a true gentleman and treated Joe's mom like a queen. Joe had decided that was the right way to live.

They all understood how important this life lesson was after that. Plus, the fact that Joe was willing to play the part of "girl" so a bunch of teenaged boys—half of which weren't even his kids—could learn the right way to act, well, it made a huge impression on Zach. Probably on all of the guys.

And so Carrie would now meet gentleman Zach. As soon as the song ended, he guided her off the dance floor, pulled out her chair for her, and offered to get her a drink. Surprisingly, Carrie didn't seem to notice the change in his behavior. She must've been more upset than she looked.

After he made sure she had enough to eat and drink (non-alcoholic), he made the rounds with her, both for support and protection from any possible confrontation with her ex. That guy had a real crafty look in his eyes. Like he was always calculating how to turn things to his advantage. Zach was not at all surprised that Edward had found another sweet young woman for a girlfriend. He seemed the kind who wanted a woman to bend to his needs, not share in a true partnership. Just thinking about Carrie with that guy made him furious.

Carrie put on a good show of smiles and friendliness for everyone despite her pain over seeing her ex. She was a strong woman. They stopped at every table to thank people for sharing in the special occasion. He didn't know anyone beyond her immediate family. Didn't matter. He was here for Carrie.

Finally they finished thanking everyone. He slid an arm around her shoulders. "Would you like to dance?" It was another slow song. Her parents were out there, along with a few other older couples.

"I'd love to," she replied.

He guided her onto the dance floor, one hand on the small of her back, then arranged them in the traditional waltz position.

She wrapped her arms around his waist, pulling him close and pressing her cheek against his chest. "I'm cold."

He pulled back to look down at her. "You want my jacket?" The temperature had dropped since sunset.

She clung to him. "No."

That was when he realized she needed comfort, not warmth. He wrapped his arms around her and swayed slowly. Though what he really wanted to do was get her home, tuck her into bed and just hold her. Huh. That was new. He couldn't ever remember wanting to hold a woman with no sex involved in the equation. Maybe Carrie was rubbing off on him—cuddling the wolf had turned the wolf into a cuddler. The truth hit him with shocking clarity, stealing his breath.

He'd fallen for her. Hard. No chance of recovery.

It should've alarmed him, but love made him stupid. Stupidly hopeful that somehow, someway they could make this work. He needed to let her know. Not now. Her mind was all tangled up with her ex. Tomorrow would be soon enough for a serious talk.

They stayed another hour, until her parents announced the party was over. They had a flight to catch to Hawaii the next day to recreate their honeymoon. Everyone laughed and cheered them on.

He took off his suit jacket and draped it over Carrie's shoulders, then walked her to his truck, one hand on the small of her back. She was quiet and he knew her well enough to know she was still hurting. "Anything I can do?" he asked.

"I'm fine."

They got to his truck and he helped her in the passenger side and shut the door. Actually he did that all the time. Guess some of his gentleman manners had trickled out without him thinking about it.

On the drive home, she broke down in quiet tears. He'd been expecting it, but it didn't make it any easier. His chest ached in sympathy. By the time he pulled into the parking lot at her place, she was wiping her eyes.

He turned off the truck. "Would you take him back right now if you could?"

"No!" Fresh tears poured out. "But it could've been me! He proposed to me! I told him no."

"C'mere."

She just kept crying, her shoulders shaking. "How did he move on so fast? Was he with her when we were together?"

He pulled her across the console and cradled her in his lap. "It doesn't matter. You don't belong with him. He made you miserable."

She sobbed into his shirt. He wrapped his arms around her, wishing he knew how to make it better for her. She spoke in a choked voice. "My mom apologized to me right after the ceremony. She didn't know about the pregnancy. Edward had kept it a secret, even from his own parents."

"I'm sorry you found out that way." He couldn't think of a single good reason why her ex would keep it secret unless the pregnancy had been a surprise to him too, sprung on him at a late date.

She sniffled, her tone laced with bitterness. "I guess now the news is out!"

He stroked her hair.

Finally she quieted and lifted her head. "I'm sorry. I ruined your shirt."

"Don't worry about it." He glanced down at his shirt with black mascara and pink lipstick along with her tears. Stupid Edward. "You know why your ex chooses such young women?"

She nodded. "I get it now. He wants to mold them."

"And you don't need molding. You're perfect just the way you are."

She started crying again.

"What?" he asked, alarmed. "Why does that make you cry?"

"I'm not perfect. I'm messed up!" She met his eyes through a sheen of tears. "Look what I'm doing with you. I used you."

"No. I'm right where I want to be."

She frowned and wiped the smudged mascara from under her eyes. "I should've been satisfied with a one-night thing, or at least just once through the list. Instead I dragged it on for more and more fucking and then revenge against that bastard and—" her voice choked "—and I'm a terrible person."

"No, you're not terrible."

"How can you say that? My life is about sex! His is about love and home and family."

His chest tightened, making it hard to breathe. Was that all he was to her? He'd thought she had real feelings for him.

The way she lit up in his arms. The way she'd included him with her friends and her family. Before he could say anything at all, she covered her face with her hands, her shoulders shaking with quiet sobs. She was in a bad place right now. Not thinking clearly.

"I'm taking you back to my place," he told her. "You shouldn't be alone tonight."

She lifted her head, her eyes watery and red. "I have Ally."

"Ally won't hold you all night."

"Okay," she said, her voice breaking. He slid her back to the passenger seat and made the short drive back to his place.

"It was a beautiful ceremony, wasn't it?" she asked as he guided her inside.

"It was. Your parents are very lucky."

"They are," she said, folding herself into him and wrapping her arms around him tight.

He hugged her back for a long moment and then did the only thing he could think of—scooped her up and carried her to bed. He stripped down to his boxers and helped her out of the dress, the strapless bra, and her heels. Then he tucked her into his side, pulled the blanket over both of them, and held her until exhaustion finally claimed her and she went limp, dropping into sleep. This time he didn't slide her to her side. Just held her, staring at the ceiling. He didn't figure he'd get much sleep, but what the hell. Carrie was hurting and it was his job to take care of her.

Tomorrow would be soon enough for their relationship talk. This wasn't just about sex. It had to be more.

He must've dozed off. He woke to an empty bed.

He slowly sat up, jaw clenched tight. She was never up before him. Her clothes and purse weren't where he'd left them on the dresser. The apartment was silent as a tomb.

"Carrie!" he barked.

Dead silence.

He swore, grabbed a pillow and flung it across the room. Then he leaped out of bed, adrenaline fueling every muscle with tension. Fight or flight. He was a fighter; Carrie chose flight. Not gonna work for him.

But first he needed fists to a punching bag, running long distance, a hard physical workout. He couldn't be held responsible for what came out of his mouth when he was this pissed off. He'd been *wronged* after he did everything right.

He ground his teeth and yanked on a shirt. He'd been there for her, holding her all night, and then she just left? Did she think that was it? That he'd just slink off, forgotten and thrown away?

Nope. Not gonna happen. Not by a long shot.

~

Carrie was home, lying on the living room sofa in her favorite summer pajamas that always made her smile because of the cute kittens wearing party hats, but nothing could make her smile today. She held a cold compress over her eyes swollen from all her tears. Ally was fussing over her, tucking her in with a blanket and then bringing over a cup of hot tea. She sat up. "Thank you."

Ally sat next to her and patted her leg. "Edward is a dick."

"I know," Carrie said. "I don't know why I'm taking this so hard. It's not like I want to be with him."

"It was a shock."

"Yes." She sipped some tea. "And I guess some part of me saw a future that I'd never have."

"You'll have a better future with a better man. Like Zach."

"Zach," she said softly. "What the hell did I do to that man? Just picked him up at a bar, handed him my wish list, and fucked him senseless for two weeks."

"Nothing wrong with that."

"Everything's wrong with that! That's not me and you know it. I don't even know who I am anymore." She stared off in the distance. "I'm lost, Ally," she whispered over the lump in her throat. "I might never find myself again."

Ally squeezed her shoulder. "You will, I promise. You're

one of the most practical people I know. Not everything is as bad as it feels right now. Okay?"

"It feels pretty shitty."

Ally sighed. "I know. You want to binge-watch *Gilmore Girls* and eat ice cream?"

"Yes," she said in a small voice. It was their little comfort tradition.

By the time dinner rolled around, she was feeling a lot better. Nothing like escaping into another world to make the present more bearable.

"Pizza?" Ally asked.

"Sure."

Ally called and put in their usual order for pepperoni and mushrooms. Only a few minutes later, the doorbell rang.

"That was fast," Ally said and went to the peephole. She turned to Carrie. "It's Zach. Are you up to seeing him?"

Carrie pushed her hair out of her face. She hadn't even brushed it. "No, I look terrible. I'm in my pajamas."

"Hurry up and get dressed!" She unlocked the dead bolt and Carrie scrambled off the sofa, taking off toward her bedroom.

She dashed inside her room and locked the door. Then she heard Ally say, "Hi there! She'll be out in just a minute."

Zach grumbled something in reply.

Carrie hurriedly stripped out of her kitten pajamas.

"Wait!" Ally exclaimed. "She's getting ready."

A knock on her door. "Carrie, I left you several messages," he boomed through the door. "We need to talk."

She stilled, surprised at both his volume and his urgent tone. "My phone was off."

"Open up."

She pulled on a bra and fumbled the straps.

"Now," he said in the deep voice of authority. She stiffened. He was *not* the boss of her.

"You will have to wait!" she barked back and adjusted her bra.

"I don't care what you look like." The knob jiggled. "Get your pretty ass out here."

Her eyes widened at the *audacity*, ordering her around and complimenting her at the same time. "My pretty ass needs some shorts." She reached for her T-shirt, slipped it over her head, and looked around for the matching shorts.

"You better not be coordinating colors and shit."

She heard Ally giggle and then suddenly quiet. Zach probably glared at her.

"Not appreciating the Neanderthal routine!" she hollered back, running to the bathroom mirror and hurriedly wetting down her hair. Her eyes were still swollen from the tears, her skin blotchy.

"Not appreciating waiting! I can pick this lock, you know."

"Just hold on!" She quickly brushed her hair. Then she grabbed her toothbrush, squeezed out some toothpaste, and turned on the water.

"Are you brushing your teeth like a good girl?"

She froze. Those were fighting words. He knew she was trying to get away from the image that had held her back for so long. And of course she was brushing her teeth. She never neglected personal hygiene. She commenced teeth brushing without bothering to reply. Would a good girl be so rude? No, she would not. She could hear Ally trying to run interference, speaking in a cheerful tone. Zach's response was a low growl.

Finally she finished, stalked across the room and opened the door. "I'm ready, okay!"

His surly expression softened the moment he met her eyes. He folded her against his chest and held her tight. Her entire body relaxed in the firm hold, the last of the tension seeping out of her.

"You know what?" Ally chirped. "I'm just going to pick up the pizza in person." She left a moment later.

Zach finally released her. "You left without saying goodbye. I was worried about you."

She searched his features, not quite believing him. "If you were that worried, you would've tracked me down earlier."

"All right, I was pissed," he said. "I needed some time to

calm down. You cry like that for hours, I try to take care of you and then you just leave?"

Her heart squeezed painfully hard at the hurt in his voice. "I'm sorry. I wasn't thinking clearly. I headed home because I wanted to curl up on my own sofa and drown my sorrows in ice cream."

He put his arm around her shoulders, led her to the sofa, and sat next to her. His eyes were sympathetic. "Did you drown your sorrows?"

"I guess. I'm not sure why it threw me so much."

He grunted. Then he leaned forward, elbows on his knees, and stared at the floor. "Carrie, I want to keep seeing each other. Just a little longer. I know you're starting grad school next week and you'll be busy, but I'm still around for a few months." He straightened and met her eyes. "I'm not ready to stop seeing you."

Her heart thudded in her ears. He sounded so sincere, so sweet. How was it that one man could hold so much caveman in him and sweetness at the same time? She must've been worn out from her crying jag because she could feel herself softening toward him, considering the possibility of something more.

"But you're leaving to go halfway across the world," she said.

His hand slid under her hair, squeezing the nape of her neck in that way he had of firm possession and affection. "We'll cross that ocean when we get to it."

"But—"

He cut her off with a kiss and her resistance crumpled. She lost herself in him, pure joy radiating through her at the closeness after their brief separation that she'd feared was permanent. His hands slid under her shirt, his mouth hard and demanding, making her moan with wanton need. She reached for his waistband and he tore his mouth from hers.

"When's Ally coming back?" he asked.

"Soon. She's just picking up pizza."

He stood, bringing her with him. "Come on. We'll go to my place."

She didn't have to think about it. She craved what he could give her, craved their joining, even as she knew she was caving to baser need. Lust made her stupid and she'd probably regret it, but not today. Today she needed him.

They walked to his place, Zach's hand on the small of her back. He stopped several times to kiss her passionately, almost like he wanted to keep her in a hyper-aroused state. Or maybe he was afraid she'd bail, but her body was already way ahead of her brain. They reached the short stretch of sidewalk that led to his door when he halted suddenly.

A tall, thin woman stood on his doorstep. Everything about her looked polished and professional and, frankly, uptight. From her dark brown hair in a smooth pageboy cut to the string of pearls around her neck to the conservative short-sleeve black dress and matching black pumps. Next to her was a large black suitcase.

Carrie's mind scrambled to reconcile the man she knew, her bad boy, her wild man traveling the far reaches of civilization, and how he could know a woman like this—sophisticated and uptight—who seemed prepared for a long visit.

"Who is that?" Carrie asked, deliriously hopeful it was his sister since they were both tall and lean, though her suddenly clammy hands told her it was most definitely not.

Zach swore and strode up to the woman, leaving Carrie behind. Not that it mattered because the woman spoke in clear crisp tones as if she wanted Carrie to hear.

"Congratulations on your fellowship," the woman said. "I also have an opportunity in Singapore. I can join you in May as soon as the semester ends."

Zach stared at the woman for a long moment before speaking in a tone that Carrie couldn't catch. He suddenly seemed to remember Carrie and crossed back to her. "I'll get rid of her. Come on."

"Who is she?" Carrie whispered. "What does she mean fellowship?"

"My ex. This'll be quick." He dragged her along.

She dug her heels in. "I don't want to meet your ex."

He stopped and gazed into her eyes. "I met yours." The

implication was clear. He'd done her a favor showing up as her date for the ex confrontation. Now she appreciated that even more because she didn't have the slightest interest in meeting his ex. In fact, she was ready to bolt.

He slid an arm around her shoulders and pulled her close. "Don't leave. You know I'll only chase you down and bring you back."

He was teasing, reminding her of the first time she bolted from his apartment and he'd carried her back inside, tossed over his shoulder. "Fine. I'll meet her, *briefly*, and then I'm going straight inside."

His voice dropped deep and low. "Where you belong."

Her stomach did a delicious flip. What this man did to her. Despite the evidence to the contrary—the woman had a suit-case like she planned to stay—she told herself to give him the benefit of the doubt. He'd deal with his ex and then return to Carrie as promised. She certainly wouldn't want to be judged by the appearance or actions of her ex.

Carrie approached the front door, a smile plastered on her face. Zach stuck close to her side and introduced her to the woman.

"Muriel, this is Carrie."

"Hi, nice to meet you," Carrie chirped. "I'm just going to head inside." She pointed around the woman to the door.

The woman grabbed her hand and shook it in a firm grip. "Dr. Muriel Hapsburg. One of Zach's colleagues at the university and more than that, as you might've guessed. A year together, quite serious."

Carrie's mind whirled. She turned to him. "You work at a university?"

Zach shoved a hand in his hair. "Yes, a professor of anthropology. I was going to tell you. Right after the anniversary celebration, but then you were crying and we just got back here. I was going to tell you," he finished lamely.

"Who does she think you are?" Muriel asked.

Carrie stared at Zach, uncomprehending, trying to recon-cile reality with what she thought she knew. And then something clicked. "That's why Josh called you professor. But you said you were a travel guide, who was currently unemployed. And then you got the Singapore gig."

"It's not a *gig*," Muriel said, emphasizing the word like it was ludicrous. "He's just been granted a senior research fellowship at the Asia Research Institute." She turned to Zach. "I assume you'll be continuing work on your book there."

He inclined his head.

Book? Shit! Josh had asked him about his book too. But Zach had said there was no book. Carrie blinked, willing herself to understand how she could've been so manipulated that she believed the man who stood in front of her. A stranger to her now. The man she thought she knew didn't exist.

"Carrie, listen," Zach said, "in a way, what I said was true. I study and write about Indonesia and the surrounding Southeast Asia region. I do spend a lot of time hiking and camping in the forest there. And I'm not actively working right now because I've been busy with you."

"In a way?" she shouted. "In what way is an anthropology professor a travel guide?"

He blew out a breath. "You're missing the point."

"I'd say she got the point just fine," Muriel said smugly.

Muriel kept talking, but Carrie couldn't hear past the roaring in her ears. Fury like she'd never known ripped through her. He'd *lied* to her. Lied about who he was. Lied about what he did. Lied about not doing long-term. *Hello, Muriel!* Not a travel guide or unemployed. She'd had the harrowing results of lies during her time with Edward and she would not tolerate them again.

"Goodbye, Zach." She headed for home on stiff legs, cold to her core, feeling like an absolute fool.

"Carrie, wait!"

She kept going.

He caught up to her and held her by the upper arm. "Carrie."

She shook him off. "Don't touch me. We're done. You lied to me."

"Let me explain."

She waited.

"Okay, it was a lie, but—"

"Zach!" Muriel called. "Can you toss me the key?"

Zach looked to the sky before barking, "No."

"Go ahead and talk to her," Carrie said. "We're done."

His light brown eyes narrowed. "Let me get this straight. Are you saying that now that you know who I really am, a respected professional in my field, you don't want me?"

She swallowed hard. This was just like her ex, lying and then turning it around like *she* was the one with the problem. She couldn't believe she'd ignored the signs, letting herself be fooled all over again. "I'm saying goodbye."

He glowered down at her. "Good luck with the next random guy you pick up. I'm done playing white knight for you." He stalked off back to his waiting ex.

"No one asked you to!" she hollered to his back.

He turned, opened his mouth and shut it with a snap. "Bye, Carrie," he muttered.

She headed for home on shaky legs. But not before she heard Muriel cry, "I'm here because I still love you!"

Carrie didn't stick around for Zach's response.

Zach took a deep breath and reached for patience as Muriel pronounced, "I'm willing to take marriage off the table to be discussed at a later date. I never should've given you an ultimatum."

"Muriel, I'm sorry. We're not getting back together."

"Because of her?" she spat.

"Not just because of her. You and I broke up more than a year ago. We've both moved on."

"But I love you!"

He didn't know what to say. He had loved her at one time, but he was in a different place. His heart was for Carrie. It was time he let Carrie know that. Though something was bothering him about this whole Muriel showing up on his doorstep thing. It was strange after more than a year. "How did you even find me?"

"I called your dad and told him how much I still loved you. I asked him not to say anything because I wanted to speak to you face-to-face and I wasn't sure if you'd let me."

He stared at her, not entirely convinced at her reasoning. "Are you going through a breakup?"

"Not exactly." She looked away. "It's very difficult to meet people at my age."

She was only a year older than him. "You're thirty-five."

Her eyes flashed. "I'm aware of how old I am! It's different for women. Men want a pretty young thing. Like that girl, Caren."

He let that slide. She purposely called Carrie by the wrong name. "Why would you want to be with me when you know I'm a lone wolf? You must not have believed I'd ever commit. You said it went back to my childhood. Did you think anything would be different this time around? I'm still the same person."

Her face crumpled. "You're not a lone wolf! I said that out of anger. I'm sorry." She sank to the porch step, buried her face in her hands, and quietly sobbed.

"But I never liked to spend the night. Remember? I couldn't sleep with you." But he'd slept with Carrie. He'd even fallen asleep holding her in his arms.

Because she was his mate.

The knowledge made the blood rush through his veins, exhilaratingly alive.

Muriel lifted her head. "Sleeping in different beds was irritating, not a deal breaker."

"So I'm not a lone wolf?" But even as he asked the question, he already knew. Yes, it was in his nature to observe, to be a little reserved, but that didn't mean he didn't have real connections. His family, Muriel for a time, and now Carrie. He was still like every other human in existence made to gather in groups for survival. He would've reached that conclusion earlier if he hadn't let his emotions cloud his thinking. The lone-wolf label had stung, made him feel like a failure, like he'd never find a relationship that lasted. Damn Muriel. Being a psychologist, she really knew how to screw with his head.

"I need to go talk to Carrie," he told her. "When I get back, I want you gone."

Her eyes still glistened with tears, her voice choked and small. "Don't you care about me at all?"

He did, once, but no more. "Goodbye, Muriel."

"Bye," she whispered. She stood and slowly wheeled her suitcase down the sidewalk.

He took off at a loping run, veering around her, eager to talk this through with Carrie because the path forward had never been clearer.

When he got to her door, he was pumped from the run and from all the bright hope for their future. He took a few deep breaths and knocked. And knocked and knocked. Then he rang the bell. Her car was parked out front. He rang the bell again. Nothing.

Then he pulled out his phone and texted her. She replied, *go away.*

"Carrie!" he hollered through the door. "We need to talk. Just give me five minutes."

The door suddenly sprang open and he started in surprise. He'd thought he'd have to work harder.

"What?" she asked.

He studied her face, no signs of crying. She was just mad. He could work with mad. "Can I come in?"

She backed up, her lips pressed in a flat line.

He stepped inside and shut the door quietly behind him. "I'm sorry I lied. I just wanted to be with you. I felt like pretending for the sake of role play, you know, the bad-boy thing, was the best way to give you the experience you wanted."

"You must've thought I was so naïve," she said, her lip curling.

"Not naïve, inexperienced. Now you're experienced."

She glared at him.

He rushed on. "I swear from here on out, complete

honesty. I'm usually very honest, I always keep my word and carry through on my promises. Ask anyone in my family."

She swallowed visibly, but said nothing. Shit. He'd hurt her even more with that. He'd basically said he only lied with her.

He reached out to stroke her arm, but she pulled away from his touch, crossing her arms. "Carrie," he said gently, "it was just because I wanted to make it good for you."

"Don't put this on me!"

He jammed a hand in his hair. "Sorry, I'm messing this up. Here's me being honest, okay? I want a relationship with you. I want long-term. I want—" he took a deep breath "—I want you to come to Singapore with me. Then when we get back to the States, I'll apply for a new job wherever you want to live."

She slowly shook her head.

His stomach dropped. She was slipping away. "Just think about it. I'm here through Christmas. You can give me an answer in a couple of months."

A heavy silence dropped between them. Her voice was subdued when she finally spoke, which was so unlike her, he knew whatever she said next would not be good. "Even if I believed that you plan to be honest from here on out, which I'm not sure I do, you know I'm starting grad school next week. Am I just supposed to drop everything and follow you around the world? Give up what I've worked so hard for? My career is important to me. I've put my own dreams on the back burner for too long because of a man and I won't make that mistake again."

"So you want me to give up my fellowship? Even though it'll probably boost my résumé enough to open up opportunities for a job at the university of my choice?"

She held up a hand. "I'm not asking you to do anything." She went to the front door and held it open, waiting for him to leave.

"Just give it some thought," he urged.

She looked at the floor and then back to him. "I'm sorry, Zach. This just isn't going to work."

He didn't know how to convince her. Her expression was

closed against him. It was so unlike her usual open warmth it made him feel cold all over. She just kept standing there, holding the front door open in an obvious request for him to leave.

He slowly walked out of her apartment, still scrambling for the words that would fix this. Nothing. He had nothing.

The door slammed shut behind him.

He stood there for a full minute just outside her door, his entire body numb with shock. One thing after another had gotten between him and Carrie. Her ex, his ex, his lies, their jobs. Maybe she was right. It just wasn't going to work.

He headed for home, his eyes watering, chest aching, limbs heavy. They'd only been together a little over two weeks, yet it hurt like hell. How had he gotten in so deep so fast?

14

———

Carrie dragged through the rest of the week, working and then crashing on the sofa, eating too much ice cream. Ally was sympathetic and supportive, but when she suggested maybe talking to Zach would help, Carrie retreated to her room. Ally didn't understand letting someone go. She still clung to the hope she'd get back together with her ex-boyfriend from college. The only thing Carrie looked forward to was the Happy Endings Book Club meeting at Something's Brewing Café on Thursday night. She needed their support. She was sure her friends would understand the pain of the betrayal, sure they'd have all the right words to reassure her that she'd done the right thing by ending it with Zach.

Thursday night finally rolled around. The first sign that things weren't going to go her way was the choice of book. The hero was a real alphahole, and as the discussion flowed over her about his redeeming qualities, all she could think about was how much Zach wasn't that kind of bad boy and how lucky she'd been to have him initiating her into erotic pleasures instead of some guy that was only in it for himself. Even pretending to be a bad boy, he'd been good to her. She felt herself softening toward him, but then she reminded herself he'd flat-out lied when she'd asked him about his job and what he was doing in Indonesia. Lied about never doing long-term too. Those were only the lies she knew about. Maybe there were more.

She looked to the ceiling, blinking rapidly at the threatening tears. She couldn't believe how attached she'd gotten to him in such a short time. It had been three days since their breakup and the emotional pain was getting worse not better.

Hailey, sitting next to her, reached over and put a hand on Carrie's arm. "What's wrong?"

She looked at Hailey—perfectly put together in a dark green designer dress with matching heels, her perfectly made-up face etched with concern, her long strawberry blond hair perfectly smooth and straight—and thought she'd never look as put together as this woman because Carrie was a mess. Inside and out. Her emotions were a tangled mess, her hair was a mess, her clothes weren't even matching. Her whole *life* was a mess and everything sucked.

Carrie looked around the room at the women who were like sisters to her and realized half of them weren't even single anymore. They were beyond this kind of heartbreak and she had a whole future full of it. There was Lauren (engaged), Mad (engaged), Charlotte (married and pregnant), even Ally was gearing up for a committed relationship with her ex. Never mind that Hailey, Missy, Sabrina, and Lexi were currently single, they'd probably all find the love of their lives before Carrie did.

Her lower lip wobbled. Ally rushed over to hug her. Hailey handed her a tissue.

"I'm sorry," Carrie said, wiping her eyes with the tissue. "It's just been a rough week."

"What happened?" Missy asked. She was a tough practical woman but great at support. "It's better to share the burden."

Suddenly she couldn't bring up Zach. Hailey had told her all along that Carrie was the one who was going to get hurt by the stupid fling idea. She couldn't bear an *I told you so*, even if said with love. Instead she focused on the other shitty thing. "You guys remember about my ex? How we were together for six years?"

"Yes," the women said in near unison notes of sympathy.

"Well, I just saw him and he's getting married and she's pregnant!"

"Oh, Carrie." Hailey stood and pulled Carrie into a hug. Then she announced, "Group hug!"

The women surrounded her, murmuring sympathies. A few moments later, they pulled apart and returned to their seats.

"Thanks, ladies," Carrie said, her voice wobbling.

"Fuck him," Mad snapped, probably the toughest of all the women. She'd been raised with a posse of big brothers and a cop dad. Her brown eyes blazed with fury on Carrie's behalf. "I mean it, Carrie. You say it too. *Fuck. Him.* He treated you shitty and you wouldn't want to be his pregnant wife anyway."

"Yeah," Ally chimed in.

"Fuck him," Carrie said, her lower lip wobbling again. She bit it.

"It's okay," Hailey said, stroking Carrie's hair. "You'll find the person for you, and when you do, you'll be his pregnant wife."

"Geez, not everyone wants the husband and kids," Missy said.

"Carrie does," Hailey returned. "Right, Carrie?"

She couldn't speak past the ball of emotion lodged in her throat. For the longest time that was what she'd wanted most of all. Now she had too much baggage to be willing to try again. Not for a long time. This only reaffirmed that she'd done the right thing calling it off with Zach. It was time to focus on her own well-being, on her dreams, her career.

She looked around at all the concerned faces of her best friends in the world and blurted, "Zach and I aren't seeing each other anymore."

"Because of your ex?" Mad asked.

Some of her previous anger returned, the pain of betrayal still fresh and bitter. "Because he lied."

Mad stiffened. "What do you mean he lied?"

Carrie shut her mouth. Zach was one of Mad's honorary brothers. Carrie should've known Mad would take his side.

"I'm sorry, Carrie," Mad said, "but Zach's not a liar. He's a stickler about being honest. You must've misunderstood."

"No, I didn't," Carrie snapped. "What, do you think I'm an idiot?"

"Carrie," someone said in a soft warning. Probably Lauren, the peacemaker.

Mad merely stared, unperturbed by her outburst.

"He pretended to be a bad boy," Carrie said. "When I asked him about his job, he said he was an unemployed travel guide." She left out the fact that he also lied when he said he didn't do long-term. It only made her look more the fool for continuing to see him. And she didn't even want to mention his crazy ex-girlfriend showing up at his door with a suitcase. Who does that?

Mad cocked her head. "What? Why would he say that?"

Ally chimed in. "Probably because she gave him a sex list she wanted a bad boy to do."

Carrie whipped her head to glare at Ally.

Ally shrugged. "Just a guess."

"Duh," Missy said. "A guy will say anything if you offer him unlimited no-strings sex."

Several of the women agreed.

Carrie stared at the ground, a sour taste in her mouth. She'd made it all too easy for him. She lifted her head and said with a bravado she was far from feeling, "So my bad, end of story."

Mad crossed her leg, her ankle over her knee. "That explains it. I saw him at Garner's just before I came here, growling at everyone like a wounded bear."

Carrie winced. "Maybe I'll skip drinks tonight." They always went to Garner's after book club for drinks. Was that why he went there tonight? She didn't want to see him. She was still too upset.

"Coward," Mad spat.

"Mad!" Hailey exclaimed.

Mad jabbed a finger at Carrie. "What? She is. She's upset; he's upset. Just fucking talk to him."

"He lied to me!" Carrie exclaimed. "He's an anthropology professor."

Mad scowled. "So fucking what. You don't want him because he's a professor? What the hell's wrong with you?"

A stunned silence fell. Their group had always been about a sisterhood of close support. Especially in broken-hearted territory.

What the hell *was* wrong with her? Why was she so upset? She wasn't broken-hearted. That would imply—

"Damn, Mad, that's harsh," Missy said. "The girl is hurting."

Mad ignored that. "You have any idea how hard he worked to get where he is today? PhD. That's four years after college plus a dissertation that's practically a book that he had to defend in front of a committee."

"I know what a PhD is!" Carrie exclaimed.

Mad went on, each word harsher than the next. "After *years* of people telling him he's a bad seed. Did he tell you how he got drop-kicked through the foster system? *Nobody* wanted him. A runaway who lied and stole his way through their homes. You know how many people told him he was a no-good ungrateful kid?"

"I didn't—" Carrie started and then stopped, her throat choked, her heart aching for the kid he used to be. She knew he'd been in foster care. She hadn't known he'd been told he was a bad seed. That kind of thing could stick with a kid, make you believe you were less than.

Mad showed no mercy. "Did he tell you how he got so street smart? How he can pick locks and break and enter with the best of them? His parents were criminals. Both of them dead from that line of work. So you tell me how someone that comes through those circumstances and fucking makes a man of himself is someone that's not good enough for you!"

"He never told me about his parents being criminals!" Carrie cried. Oh, God. She wanted to hug him. He hadn't shared much about himself. But had she asked?

"Of course he wouldn't," Mad snapped. "You judged him for the good stuff he's done. How's he ever supposed to trust you enough to tell you the bad stuff?"

She blinked rapidly, not wanting to break down again, but the tears came anyway.

"That's enough, Mad," Hailey said. "I know he's your blood brother, but Carrie is hurting. She's our friend. Besides, you shouldn't be sharing Zach's personal issues here. That's for a private conversation." Hailey took them all in. "What happens at book club, stays at book club. Right, ladies?"

The women murmured their agreement.

An uncomfortable silence fell. Several of her friends gave her sympathetic looks.

"Sorry, Carrie," Mad muttered.

Carrie shook her head. The apology was unnecessary and not sincere anyway. Everything she thought she knew about Zach shifted once more. From sexy bad boy to anthropology professor to troubled kid. There were so many sides to him and she was drawn to all of them. But was it just empathy she had for him, or was it more?

Hailey piped up. "On that note, who wants chocolate?"

Everyone raised their hand.

"We'll go back to my place instead of Garner's," Hailey said. "Okay, Carrie?"

Carrie nodded numbly.

But when they wrapped up the meeting and headed out, Carrie changed her mind. "You go without me. I'm going to Garner's to talk to Zach."

"We'll go with you," Hailey said. "We've got your back. Every one of us." She shot Mad a look.

Mad sighed. "I got your back too. But you understand I love Zach. He's family."

"Understood," Carrie said.

"I'm sorry I was harsh," Mad said. "You know you're my sister." She fist-bumped her. "Now go get him."

~

Zach was on whiskey number three when he heard the feminine murmur of a crowd of women. Josh had already warned him that Carrie would be here tonight with her friends. He'd been counting on it. He had a thing or two to get off his chest. Like how she belonged with him. Like how much she'd love Singapore if she just gave it a chance. Gave *him* a chance. He deserved that much, didn't he?

He turned and saw her—her face an expression of pure sympathy. Fuck. Did he look as bad as he felt?

She stopped in front of him and said in a soft voice, "Mad told me about your parents being criminals. I'm so sorry." She tried to hug him, but he leaned back.

He stared at her, read the pity in her eyes, and scowled. "That wasn't her story to tell."

"She was defending you. Telling me how much you've overcome to get where you are today."

All the old shit rang through his head. *He's a bad seed. You can't trust him. Sneaky, a liar and a thief.* He could never get away from it. Now Carrie knew. She'd always see him through that lens.

"Zach—"

"I don't want your pity," he snarled.

"I had no idea. Of course I don't think badly of you for it."

He narrowed his eyes. "But that's what you see now. A bad seed that worked out of the pit."

"But it's a good thing. You're amazing."

He stared down at her, looking for any signs of love, but all he saw was pity. "I'll never be a good seed, Carrie. Get that through your head. No matter how hard I worked to improve my social status." He swiped a hand through the air. "Education. PhD. Research. Nothing changes where I came from. What I am on a cellular level. So…" He turned back to the bar and threw back the rest of the whiskey. It burned down to his gut. Good.

"Zach." Her gentle voice just pissed him off more.

He turned back to her. "Guess you did get a bad boy. Bad, bad, *bad*. Can't trust that one. Ironic that you hated all the shiny trappings." He laughed mirthlessly. "Maybe you always saw through that. Your dad asked about my people. Here's your answer. Be sure to tell your dad." He leaned close. "My people come from organized crime. Sophisticated, well-planned illegal operations. Drugs, money, jewels. That's what took my mom. Jewels and bam! Gone. Execution style."

Her blue eyes widened.

"Yup." He leaned back, a little light-headed from too much whiskey and too little food. Not enough whiskey in the world for this kind of pain. Heartache. It just dug at you relentlessly. He turned back to the bar, lifted his empty glass and shook it at Josh. "'Nother one."

"You've had enough." Josh said, putting a bowl of pretzels in front of him. "Eat."

He lifted a pretzel and stared at it. Two interlocking loops like a heart. He snapped it in half.

"Zach!" Carrie exclaimed.

He turned, surprised at her volume. "What?"

"Look, I'm not sure what all that status stuff means to you, but to me it's not important. I don't think you're a bad seed at all. You were my white knight just like you said. You kept me safe for what could have been some very risky behavior with any other random guy I picked up."

He stared at her. She was saying all the right things, but her blue eyes were soft with sympathy, like she wanted to hug him and make him all better. She was seeing him all wrong now and he hated it. He'd worked hard to become more than his past. It always bit him in the ass.

"You can't fix me," he growled.

Her voice was soft and soothing. "I was lucky to find you. And I'm so sorry you were ever told you were anything but exactly what you are—a good person. The best." She rubbed his arm.

He ignored her touch, meant in sympathy he didn't want or need.

She kept right on talking, her voice louder, more urgent, the words bouncing around his muddled head full of pain and whiskey. "I've missed you terribly. I let my ex and his lies get in my head and it messed with what we had. Can we try to start again?"

So much messed up. Didn't know how to fix it. He tossed some bills on the bar. "You know what? Neither one of us is cut out for this. You're screwed up by that asshole; I'm just screwed up." He stood unsteadily. "I'm going home."

He took one step and the room tilted.

"Josh!" a woman hollered. Not Carrie. He focused with great effort. Hailey with the light red hair. Pretty.

"On it," Josh said, coming around the bar. He put an arm around Zach. "I'm driving, big guy." He turned and called, "Mad, take over for me." Mad was a part-time bartender at the place. Little Mad, the only little sister Zach had ever known.

"Bye, shortstack!" he called.

"Bye, Professor!" Mad returned with real affection. See, people thought he was cool with all his studying.

"We'll talk later, okay?" Carrie asked, appearing at his side. "Tomorrow."

He'd talk right now. "I was bad in *exactly* the way you wanted me to be. You couldn't get enough. All night, every night, every fuck—" He was cut off when Josh jerked him away. He stumbled and then looked over his shoulder at Carrie, her eyes still filled with sympathy. "Take your sympathy home with you and leave it there!"

"Enough," Josh snapped, dragging him toward the back door that led to the parking lot.

Good old Josh. He had an identical twin, Jake, and Zach still hadn't seen his old friend. "I'm fine, Josh, dude, bro. When's Jake coming back?"

"Zach, dude, bro, you're not safe behind the wheel. Only reason I've been serving you is to keep an eye on you. Now you're cut off. And Jake'll be back next weekend."

"I miss Jake. He's neater than you."

"You're the best kind of drunk. Goofy."

They stepped outside. Zach was not feeling goofy, he was feeling wounded, fucking heartbroken. Doomed to be a lone wolf forever, whether he chose that path or not. He threw his head back and howled at the moon.

Surprisingly, Josh joined in.

He stopped to stare at him. "Are you a lone wolf too?"

Josh grinned. "Yeah, bro, I'm a lone wolf too." He snagged Zach, one hand on the back of his neck, and walked him to his car, a black Miata convertible.

"Your car's too small for my legs."

"You're an inch taller than me. I think you'll fit."

Carrie always thought he was so-o-o tall, but obviously he was only an inch taller than Josh's six feet. She was just short. Petite.

Josh opened the passenger-side door and gave him a shove to get in. He did, pulling the seat back as far as it would go. Stupid convertible. Josh should get a real man's car. Like a truck.

Josh got in and started the car.

"She's judging me," Zach informed him.

"They do that." He pulled out of the lot.

He slapped the dashboard. "Pitying me!"

"Nah."

"Ask her!"

Josh gave him a small slap of brotherly affection on the cheek. "We'll talk when you're sober."

They drove in silence, his own thoughts dark and getting worse. Who was Carrie to judge him just because she came from perfect la-la land of perfect married parents in perfect suburbia somewhere. He didn't even know where. He knew next to nothing about her except for her taste and her softness and her sounds, like when she came or when she got excited to see him or when she ate something delicious. He sighed at the memory.

Josh walked with him to his front door. Zach pulled out his keys, unlocked the door, and turned to Josh. "Sometimes when she sleeps, she whimpers like a kitten. Like something's bothering her and then I just stroke her hair, pet her like that —" he petted his own hair "—and she stretches out content and quiet."

"Awesome. I don't want to see you drinking again." Josh poked him in the chest. "Be a man and face whatever's crawled up your ass."

"It's her!"

"Then face *her*. When you're sober."

"Who do you think you are?" he snarled, but Josh didn't have a good answer. He just reached over, pushed open the door, and shoved him inside.

"Wuss!" Zach yelled through the closed door.

"Sleep it off, bonehead!"

He stumbled to the sofa and lay down because Carrie had *ruined* the bed for him. Too many memories of his little kitten, his tigress, his pussy. Fucking *hell* he missed her.

15

Carrie headed to her apartment the next night after work, depressed that she hadn't heard from Zach. She understood him so much better now, where he came from, how hard he'd worked to achieve something admirable, the different sides of him. And they'd been good together. Good was an understatement. She climbed the steps to her second-floor apartment. She'd wanted to try to work something out. Obviously he didn't want the same thing. Too many goodbyes in her life right now. Goodbye to Zach. Goodbye to her work family, whom she'd grown to love over the last four years. Tomorrow, Saturday, was her last shift at work. Grad school started on Monday.

She stopped short and sucked in a breath to find Zach standing on her doorstep. He studied her in his serious way like she was the most fascinating person he'd ever met. Her heart soared. In that moment she knew there was no getting around what she felt for him, no matter how scary it was to take that risk. No matter how difficult it would be to do the long-distance thing. They'd make it work. She hoped.

"Hi," she said.

He gazed directly into her eyes. "I'm sober."

"I know."

He offered his hand, palm up. "I want to show you something at my place."

She had a feeling she knew what that was and she'd really like to shower before they hit the sheets. She didn't even try to fight her natural impulse to join with him again. "Give me twenty minutes to get ready."

"No."

"No?" she echoed.

"It's important."

She had a quick battle with herself. "I smell like the hospital." At least she was out of her scrubs in a simple black tank top and matching shorts.

He waited, still offering his palm to her. An open gesture of invitation. Affection. Companionship. Even with everything they'd done together, they'd never held hands. It felt sweetly romantic, like the beginning of a relationship. It was that primal language they spoke that they both instinctively understood.

She placed her hand in his.

He closed his eyes for a moment. "Thank you."

He entwined his fingers with hers and headed down the stairs. Zach was quiet on their walk, his hand warm and firm in hers.

"Are you going to give me a hint?" she asked.

"No."

The silence stretched between them.

When they were nearly at his place, she blurted, "I think we need to have a serious talk."

"We will. After I show you…something."

Her mind raced. What could it be? She'd already seen his *something*. "Are you going to show me your professor clothes? Tweed blazer with elbow patches?"

He stopped and glowered down at her, looking all hot and alpha and ready to prove himself. "I'm not a nerdy academic. There are levels and I'm at the top of the cool badass ladder."

She bit back a smile. "I know that very well." She took a deep breath, serious now. "I can understand why you let me think you were just a bad-boy traveler kind of guy. I wanted you to be this fantasy and you made it good for me."

He lifted their joined hands and kissed her fingers. "I was always me underneath that. Truth is, I was more me as a bad boy in the bedroom than I've ever been with anyone. I used to always hold back so I wouldn't come off as too aggressive."

She cocked her head. "So you're saying if we hopped into bed right now, everything would be exactly like it was? You're an alpha-bad-boy professor?" She stifled a laugh, still having trouble reconciling the two.

He narrowed his eyes. "This is serious."

"I know." She fought back a hysterical giggle, all the tension piling up in her from the ups and downs of the past week reaching a breaking point. But then she remembered his other lie, which had hurt a lot more. "What was the deal with no long-term? And there's Muriel! Were you just trying to let me down easy? Were there other lies?"

He spoke in a deep even tone, meeting her gaze directly. "No, there are no more lies. I swear on my life. And you can ask me anything else you want to know about me and I promise to answer honestly *after* I show you something."

She parked a hand on her hip. "What about the no long-term thing?"

His eyes took on a determined gleam, which made her suddenly wary.

"Uh, Zach—ah!" He'd tossed her over his shoulder. "Zach!"

He grunted and gave her bottom a pat. "I told you we'd have our serious talk after I show you something."

Her body flushed with heat. "Ah, carry on."

He carried her down the sidewalk to his front door and set her on her feet. Then he gazed into her eyes, kissed her fast and hard, and released her. "After you."

He opened the door and let her in.

Everything looked the same to her. Same black sofa, same TV, same pile of boxes.

He took her hand and walked her down the hallway toward his bedroom.

"I thought we were going to have a serious talk."

"After your gift," he said patiently.

Clearly he wasn't turned on like she was from the primal caveman hold. Something had tripped inside her during her time with Zach, an out-of-control need to have him close with nothing between them, skin on skin. So why was she babbling about a serious talk? It was like she was trying to convince herself to talk when all she wanted to do was strip naked and throw herself at him.

He led her to his bed and pointed at it. "Part one."

She sucked in a quick breath. "That's my comforter." Her sage green comforter was on her side of the bed. It was queen-size, so it didn't quite fit across the king-size mattress. His side had his usual navy blue blanket. "How did you—"

"Ally helped me. Come on, part two." He took her hand and led her to the bathroom and opened the medicine cabinet.

Her jaw dropped. Her stuff was in there. Her contact solution and assorted lotions and potions she enjoyed in her small beauty routine. She pressed a hand to her chest, where her heart thundered.

"Shower too," he said.

She crossed to the shower and peered through the glass shower door, where she found her shampoo, conditioner, and body wash. She slowly turned back to him, her legs wobbly, the roar of her own heartbeat pounding in her ears.

He closed the distance between them. "Do you understand?" he asked gently.

She grabbed his hand in a tight grip. "Are we moving in together? Because that feels long-term. Is this the part where you explain about not doing long-term with me?"

He gazed at her steadily. "I said that because I didn't want to lead you on, knowing I was leaving the country." He gestured to the medicine cabinet and shower. "This is symbolic."

Her brows knit together, waiting for an explanation because symbolism wasn't going to solve the fact that they would be on opposite sides of the world for a very long time.

He guided her back to the bedroom, where he offered her

a seat on his side of the bed. He took a seat next to her and took her hand in both of his. "Carrie." His voice was gravelly. "We're two good people, who are compatible sexually, and now I'd like to build on a layer of courtship starting today."

"A layer of...courtship?"

"Yes."

"And that means?"

"You're special to me, Carrie." He paused, gazing at her with deep affection, maybe even...love. Her heart thumped hard. "I'm putting you first in my life. Your dreams, your career, your happiness comes first. You're going to grad school. I'll be here with you."

Her breath caught. "But what about your fellowship in Singapore?"

"I turned it down."

She gasped. "Zach! I don't want you to give up your dreams for me. That's not right either."

"I don't need a fellowship to be happy." He released her hand and stroked her hair back from her face. "I need you."

She pressed her palms to her flushed cheeks, her heart racing. She'd never expected him to sacrifice for her. "I'm not sure—"

"*I'm* sure."

Her eyes welled, overwhelmed with this shocking wonderful news. "But won't you be burning a bridge, turning them down?"

"I explained the timing was bad. There's a wait list, anyway, so it worked out. Besides, it'll give me more time for this book I'm working on. Maybe after that I'll study something closer to home." A smile played over his lips. "I'm particularly interested in courtship rituals in modern society."

She stared at him—giddy and amazed and shocked. So shocked. Her bad-boy professor was so much better than any fantasy she could ever have dreamed up. She let out a small laugh of pure wonder, scarcely believing it.

He took both her hands in his. "I'll be here for the full year sabbatical, working on my book. I hope you'll be with me.

During that time, I'll apply for jobs locally. Columbia, Yale, and NYU all have excellent anthropology departments."

She still couldn't believe it. "You'd do that? Switch jobs for me?"

He framed her face with his large hands. "I'd do anything for you. I love you, Carrie."

She wrapped her arms around him and burrowed her head into his neck, suddenly shaky with the risk she was about to take. He stroked her back, quietly soothing her, somehow reading her in that primal language he was so good at. Tears welled up, spilling down her cheeks. A few moments later, she untangled herself from him to wipe her eyes.

She took a deep quavering breath. "I'm scared, but…I want to give us a chance."

He hugged her tight. "I won't hurt you. Promise." He pulled back, his eyes burning into hers. "Complete honesty. Complete commitment." He paused. "That is, if you're okay with not exploring more. I know you haven't dated much."

She stared at him. "You'd really let me date other men just to explore?"

His expression was fierce. "This is where my wrestling skills and physical prowess would come into play. You'd ultimately see I was the more viable partner."

"I think I already see that."

He peeled her off and stood, looking disgruntled. "You *think*?"

She grinned and stood close to him. "You could show off your physical prowess a bit more to remind me."

He flashed a devilish smile and lifted her by the waist, wrapping his arms around her. She automatically wrapped her arms and legs around him.

"You're about to meet Harvey," he growled, walking with her toward the adjacent wall.

Her back connected with the wall. *Hello, Harvey Wallbanger, my old friend.*

She giggled. "I found my viable partner."

Zach didn't make any move, though, merely pressed

against her and gazed into her eyes with so much love her eyes filled with happy tears.

She cupped his face in her hands. "I love you too. I never was a fling girl at heart."

A wide smile slowly spread across his handsome face. "The next step is I spend time with your family."

"There are steps?"

"Courtship rituals are well established throughout the history of man. One of them dictates you're not just marrying your partner, you're marrying their family. You already know my family, the Campbells, so next I need to get to know yours."

She couldn't help her smile. This was a new side to him— the academic, though she'd seen glimpses of it. Some of the things he'd said before that sounded odd now made sense. Like when he'd asked if she'd done research for her wish list or when he'd explained that everything came down to biology. And he was talking marriage, which filled her with a joy she could barely contain. She wanted to dance around the room, but she was pressed between a hard wall and a deliciously hard man. She stroked his scruffy beard, not grown in much, less wild looking but still just as dear to her. "What're the other steps?"

He set her on her feet and spoke in a confident tone. "The male has to prove he'll be a good protector through feats of strength and endurance." He paused, looking thoughtful. "It would be easier if I had some competition to wrestle."

"You could wrestle Edward."

His eyes narrowed. "You still into him?"

"No, but it would be fun to watch. I'm sure you'd kick ass."

He nodded. "My size and deep voice also give me an advantage. They indicate dominance and, therefore, protection."

She slipped her hands under his shirt and felt him up from abs to chest. "Uh-huh, keep talking, Professor."

He obliged. "Gifts are very important. The gift of food, but any gift that indicates the male will be a good provider. The only exception is matriarchal societies, which are few and far between. In that case, the gifts are given to the male."

Her hands stilled. That was cool. "Like what?"

"Flowers, jewelry, sweets, or larger items like livestock, property, a house. I'd like to buy you a house."

Her jaw dropped. "Zach!"

He tipped her chin up, closing her jaw. "Don't look so surprised. I'm a good provider living modestly. My savings are decent."

She kissed him. "Your academic talk is getting me hot."

He flashed a smile and cupped her ass, holding her against him. "I wear long-sleeve button-down collared shirts with dress pants and a belt to work."

She laughed. "Of course you do. What else?"

He nipped her bottom lip. "I'll likely be offering you love letters and/or poems. If you find all of these acceptable, and you don't mind where I came from—"

"I don't."

"Then you should know I will also be a suitable procreative partner. Healthy virile male." His brows furrowed, deep in thought, before he concluded, "That about covers it." He cradled her jaw, stroking lightly across her cheek. "You light up my world, Carrie. You're my mate."

My mate. Her heart squeezed at the odd but perfectly Zach phrasing and she melted, just melted, legs quivering, actually weak at the knees. She clung to him, her throat nearly closed with the huge ball of emotion lodged there. Love, it was *love.* She never thought she'd find it again. "That is the sweetest thing anyone has ever said in the history of the universe! You're going to make me cry." A tear escaped that he wiped away with his thumb. "You're my mate too!"

He hugged her for a long moment, cupping her head to his chest. She let out a shuddering breath, relaxing again safe in his arms.

He pulled back far enough to meet her eyes. "If you're not ready to move in with me, I'll put your stuff back. It was symbolic, that gesture, though I'd love to have you here with me." He kissed her and spoke against her lips. "Where you belong."

He pulled away so suddenly, she was dazed for a moment. He studied her, seeming to be waiting for her to say something.

"Are my clothes already in your dresser?" she asked.

He went to the dresser and opened three drawers. Completely empty. "I made room, but I didn't want to be presumptuous. Just brought enough over to drive the symbolism home. I want you in my life."

She clapped a hand over her mouth, her eyes stinging. He studied her in his observant way, watching with an intensity that told her exactly how important she was to him. She turned, walked a few steps away, then ran and leaped at him. He caught her and she peppered him with kisses all over his face. A zillion suns burst through her in euphoric joy.

"Is that a yes to moving in?" he asked with a laugh.

"Yes! I love you! Yes!" She rubbed her cheek against his beard, practically purring in contentment. Then she lifted her head to find him smiling that rare sweet smile that made her heart sing. "You're so sweet. I never knew how sweet. I'd swoon at your feet if you weren't holding me."

He snapped his teeth at her. "I'm a wolf. Watch yourself."

A hot shiver raced down her spine. "You're so much better than any fantasy I could ever dream up. You're like a dream come true."

They gazed into each other's eyes, the unspoken connection more powerful than all the words in the world.

She kissed him again. "Now, Professor, tell me all about your research." She wanted to understand that side of him.

He set her back on her feet and lifted a finger in full professor mode. "That would actually help me a lot. I've been wanting to bring my work to a nonacademic audience. If I can explain it to a nonanthropologist like yourself, and you understand it, I'll know I'm on the right track. I just need to unpack everything from my wall of boxes and organize it as a whole. Give me a week on that."

She beamed. It seemed when it was a topic dear to his

heart, he had a lot to say. "Okay. Now that we're being completely honest, what did you think of me when I handed you my wish list, thinking you were a bad boy? Did you think I was a naïve idiot?"

"No." He stroked her hair back from her face and then cradled her jaw, his gaze tender. "I read between the lines."

"And?" she whispered.

"I knew what you really wanted."

"And what was that?"

He shifted his hand, stroking his thumb across her lower lip. "It wasn't passion, though you were sorely in need of that experience."

"Tell me."

"Everything on your wish list was focused on you because you wanted to feel special."

"I did?"

"Yes. Your ex made you feel less than, so your secret desire was to feel special." He pulled his phone from his jeans pocket and tapped a few times, pulling up the list. "Okay, take number one. Dessert comes first." He met her eyes. "Besides the obvious sexual euphemism, it says I want to come first with you. I want to feel special. See?" He looked down at his phone again. "And this next one. Top floor. I would like to be important to you. High on top. I want to feel special." He lifted his head. "See how it comes back to that?" He rattled the next few off in a rapidly rising voice. "Sunday drive, can't even keep my hands off you in a car because you're so damn special; squeaky clean, can't stop touching you even in my personal time—"

She cut him off. "You're brilliant!" Her cheeks burned, embarrassed that he'd seen right through her, delving deep to what even *she* hadn't realized she wanted. No other man would've taken that list and read so deeply into it. He was amazing. Utterly amazing.

"Here's another one," he said. "Animals are primal. I want to feel alive in my skin. I want to feel—"

"Special," she finished for him. He seemed to enjoy

figuring out the puzzle of Carrie. She liked it too since he was so good at it.

He kept going with extra enthusiasm. "Yes! The focus is on you so you feel special. And what does meeting Harvey, a wallbanger, represent?" He raised his brows. "Strength on your partner's part to lift and hold you for a duration of time, but also your partner would be overcome with passion, face-to-face, focus on you. And, of course, Jane Bond can't help but have the focus on her since she's tied up." He shoved the phone back in his pocket and grinned. "I like that last one a lot."

She flew into his arms and kissed him. This time his focus was back on her and he took over the kiss, gripping her hair, his lips hard and demanding, his tongue thrusting inside. She mewled in the back of her throat, already hot and wet and ready. His other hand cupped her ass and slid between her legs, igniting her. She pulled at his shirt, desperate for skin on skin, but was still caught in his hold. Just when she was about to demand he rip his clothes off, he lifted his head, gazing into her eyes.

"Do you agree with my interpretation?" he asked in his gruff and growly voice.

"Yes, you're so observant," she said in a breathy voice.

He kissed her gently. "I am. For you and everyone else but not myself. All this time I thought I wasn't good at relationships, but I was just waiting for you." He lifted a hand and cradled her jaw. "You're special to me." His voice was gruff with emotion. "More than I ever imagined someone could be. You're it for me, Carrie."

Her eyes stung, overwhelmed once more by the love pouring out of him. All for her. "I can't believe you read between the lines to what I really needed. I didn't even know I was putting that in there until you said it."

He gave her a small smile. "Takes a special someone to see, an anthropologist type."

She framed his face with her hands. "A good man."

He turned his head and nipped her palm. "I'll still be your bad boy in the bedroom. That comes naturally."

"No holding back."

He kissed her. "Couldn't if I wanted to." He scooped her up, carried her to the bed, and lowered her to the mattress, but he didn't join her right away. Instead he stood, gazing down at her before flashing a brilliant smile. "You are *the* woman, Carrie Young. I've been looking for you." She recognized her pickup line from weeks ago.

She held out her arms to him. "Yeah? Where've you been looking?"

He climbed on top of her, resting on his forearms, and spoke in a husky voice. "Everywhere."

She wriggled under him. "Rip my clothes off, bad boy, and have your wicked way with me."

He obliged because he was a very *good* bad boy. Once they were both naked, he settled between her legs but didn't take her in his usual hard thrust. Instead he slid in slowly and then stilled. He cradled her cheek with one hand and gazed into her eyes.

"Carrie," he rasped in a voice thick with emotion.

"Yes," she whispered.

"I have a wish list. One thing on it."

She ran her fingers through his short hair and then across his shoulders. "Tell me."

He didn't reply, merely shifted, kissing along her jawline as he made love to her, taking her slow and deep. Her head dropped back and he nuzzled along the side of her neck.

He kissed her and spoke against her lips. "I want all of you."

"Yes," she whispered, wrapping her arms and legs tight around him. "You have me. All of me."

He got more aggressive then, pumping hard and fast in what felt like a claiming. Her fingernails dug into his shoulders, hanging on for the ride. He slipped a hand under her hip, lifting her to take him deeper. She moaned as the pressure built within her. And then his eyes locked on hers and her breath hitched, her heart racing as she read in his eyes what he really wanted from her.

"Zach, I love you unconditionally with everything I am."

His eyes watered and then he surged into her, his mouth crashing over hers. The intensity ratcheting up with the most powerful force of all—love.

And then she flew, coming apart safe in his arms, holding him through his own shuddering climax. He gave her his weight and they stayed like that, tangled up in each other. Merged in body and heart.

EPILOGUE

The past month of living with Zach had been nothing short of amazing. She was crazy in love. Her family loved him. Her friends thought he was awesome. Probably because he invited them over for a gourmet dinner, which he prepared. He'd lived up to his promise of total honesty, even when that meant telling her that her chicken was way overcooked or that she had a real cover hog problem (stealing his as well as hers). And his word was something she could count on. Her heart was so full.

Zach parked in the lot behind Garner's and they walked inside, hand in hand, for Hailey's special night. It was the pinnacle of a wedding planner's career to be featured in *Bride Special*, a national magazine catering to upscale weddings. Hailey had an interview and photo shoot going on right now at Ludbury House, the mansion in town where weddings were held, and had invited all of their friends to Garner's afterward, where she planned to take the reporter and photographer to dinner and cocktails in a carefully controlled environment. Hailey wanted to make sure *Bride Special* readers would know how easily they could feel right at home in the warm and friendly Clover Park community. Hailey had even arranged for Logan Campbell to meet her here in the role of "boyfriend." It was, of course, a fake boyfriend, but what else was a single wedding planner to do? Hailey chose Logan because she deemed him to be the last single Campbell and had specifically wanted a Campbell because of their large close-knit family. Never mind that Josh Campbell was also single. He wasn't "eligible" on account of being a scoundrel. Ha!

Zach rested his hand on the small of her back and guided her to one of several high-topped tables set in the open area of the bar for a predinner cocktail hour. He leaned down to her ear. "I love you in this dress." She wore a sleeveless pink dress that emphasized her cleavage. Zach was a big fan of her cleavage. Hailey had suggested they all dress up in case the photographer decided to include some impromptu casual shots.

She looked up at him and smiled. "Thank you." She took in his still-not-long-enough beard and focused on his navy blue tie. "And you look very handsome."

He grinned and tipped her chin up. "I promise it'll grow back."

"I know," she said forlornly. She dearly missed his full beard—the way it rubbed so deliciously against her and how wild it made him look.

"They're serving champagne at the bar," Zach said. "Want some?"

That was odd. She thought it'd be the usual full bar. Maybe Hailey wanted to give it an extra special wedding reception feel. "Sure, why not?"

"I love that attitude," he said, gazing into her eyes in that deep loving way he had that brought shivers of happiness all the way to her toes. "*Why not* is a great way to live."

"It's new for me, but I like it too."

They smiled at each other in their newfound giddy love state before he slowly backed away. "Be right back," he said and went to fetch the champagne.

She looked around and spotted Ally with their friends. Nearly all of the Campbells and their honorary brothers were here, except their dad, who was likely babysitting his grand-daughter, Viv, so Alex and Lauren could be here. She glanced to the dining area, where a few families were eating and a table was waiting with reserved signs on it for Hailey and the magazine people. An older woman with white blond hair smiled and waved at her.

She squinted. Wait. Was that her mom? What was her mom doing here? She didn't think Hailey knew her parents. She leaned forward. Yup. That was definitely the back of her dad's head. He turned and waved.

She lifted her hand in a small wave but didn't join them since Zach was heading toward her with two glasses of champagne.

He handed over her glass and then clinked his glass against hers. "To the value of tradition."

She cocked her head, studying him. "Dr. Harrison, why are we drinking to tradition?" She used the formal address whenever he sounded overly academic.

He winked. "Nothing more traditional than planning a wedding."

She supposed that was true and they were here to cele-brate Hailey, the ultimate wedding planner. She took a sip of champagne and glanced over to her parents, where her... brother? Yes, that was definitely her brother setting two glasses of champagne in front of her parents. He then quickly returned to another table, where he sat with his wife and two daughters.

She slowly turned to Zach. "Did you invite my whole family to Hailey's big night?"

"You remember how I told you it's important to get to know the family and community of the woman you're serious about?"

"Yeah?"

He lifted his glass and spoke around it. "There's your answer." His eyes sparkled with good humor and she wondered if he was playing a joke on her, but, honestly, he wasn't much for elaborate jokes. He had more of a quick-witted, on-the-spot kind of humor.

"Okay." She drank some more champagne when Zach stopped her, his hand over hers. "What?"

"Now don't get pissed off—"

"Why would I get pissed off?"

"Because you can't hold your liquor and I'm going to ask you to please save the rest for a toast when Hailey arrives."

She stared at him blankly. "It's one glass. Can't I just get a second glass for the toast?"

He merely watched her through hooded eyes. It was both sexy and effective.

"Fine," she muttered. "Geez, pick up one random guy in a bar, hand him your sex list, and suddenly you can't get liquored up anymore."

He chuckled and kissed her. "I was in the right place at the right time."

She grinned. "Definitely."

Just then the door burst open and Hailey sailed in, laughing at something the photographer had said. She was a vision in a lavender cocktail dress with matching heels. The reporter, a woman with a dark cap of hair in her fifties with a killer body in a tight white dress, listened intently to their conversation.

Hailey stopped and looked around for Logan, who made no move to step away from the bar. "I can't wait for you to meet my boyfriend. He's a dream."

"Right here, princess," Josh said, coming up behind Hailey and dropping an arm over her shoulders. Total stealth move. Carrie hadn't even noticed him approach.

Neither had Hailey. She stiffened and then pasted on her beauty queen smile.

"Uh-oh," Carrie whispered to Zach. The entire room had hushed since everyone knew their rocky frenemy history.

Josh whispered something in Hailey's ear and they headed to the reserved table for dinner with the reporter and photographer.

This night just got weirder and weirder. First Zach went into professor mode at a party, then he gave her champagne but wouldn't let her drink it, and then Josh became an attentive fake boyfriend. Not to mention her family was here. She went to go say hi, but Zach stopped her, pulling her close and kissing her breathless.

He released her and she wobbled, blinking in surprise at him. He turned her, pointing out the next strange thing. Tuxedoed waiters filed out from the kitchen with trays of hot appetizers. They mingled among the guests, serving them up. This was so much fancier than she thought it'd be just to show the magazine people they had a welcoming community.

Zach held her champagne when she helped herself to a piece of bruschetta topped with diced tomatoes. He left and returned a moment later with a glass of water for her. He ate nothing. Merely stood there holding both of their champagne glasses.

Finally after she'd had her fill of appetizers and finished her water, she got tired of Zach holding her champagne hostage and demanded it back. He turned and crooked his finger at Hailey, who made an eating gesture.

Zach held the champagne flute to Carrie's lips. "One sip."

She sipped. "You're acting very strange tonight. Let's go say hi to my family."

"I told them we'd talk after their meal."

"Oh." She stared at him, feeling like she was missing something here. Zach watched her with hooded eyes, still holding both of their nearly full glasses of champagne. Now why did he get her champagne if he was just going to hold it hostage all night?

The tuxedoed waiters made another round among the guests, this time with champagne.

"Look," she told Zach, "everyone's on their second glass and I've only had two sips of my first. I'm completely sober."

He grunted. "Good."

Hailey appeared next to her suddenly and snagged two glasses of champagne from a passing waiter. "Hi, Carrie!" she said extra enthusiastically.

"Hi. How'd your interview go?"

Hailey met Zach's eyes and smiled. "Good. It's still going a bit."

"How's Josh at the fake boyfriend gig?"

Hailey groaned, met Josh's eyes from across the room and jerked her head in a gesture of *get over here*. "He's laying it on thick."

Josh headed over and the reporter and photographer followed at a distance.

"So what did he whisper that made you agree to let him stand in for Logan?" Carrie asked.

Josh appeared at Hailey's side and stood there, listening.

Hailey handed him a glass of champagne. "He said the interview felt like an emergency situation. As in, we only speak during emergencies. Really, Josh. I don't think they believed a word that came out of your mouth."

Josh smiled pleasantly. Probably because the photographer had his giant camera with the zoom lens out. "Why not? I do think you've done a fantastic job building your business."

Hailey's eyes widened. "You meant that? You sounded like you were teasing."

"Why? Because I smiled after I said it?"

"I thought you were smirking."

Josh shook his head and muttered, "You always think the worst."

Hailey smiled and spoke through her teeth, "Not like you don't give me good reason."

Josh made a gallant bow. "Well, princess, you're welcome. Always here to stand in for your single-lady needs." He smirked. "That'll be five hundred large."

Hailey growled.

Josh laughed out loud.

"Cad," Hailey muttered. She recovered quickly, turning and speaking loud enough to be heard over the din of conversation. "Come on, everybody! Gather close. I'd like to make a champagne toast."

A few minutes later, all of their friends had gathered close and Carrie's family too.

Hailey lifted her glass and announced, "A toast."

Zach handed Carrie her champagne and then crossed to

Hailey's side, who immediately stepped back. He then shocked the hell out of Carrie when he made the toast instead. "This toast is to Carrie Young, a woman who's so pure of heart. Beautiful inside and out."

"Zach," she whispered over the lump in her throat, "what're you doing?"

"Toasting you," he said, taking a sip of champagne and watching her over the rim.

She sipped too. Someone took the glass from her hand.

Zach gave her a tender smile and took them all in. "I've gotten to know Carrie's parents, her brother and his beautiful family, as well as all the friends we're both lucky to have in our lives. I've received her parents' blessing for this union. Now there's only one thing left to do for the culmination of the courtship ritual."

Carrie's knees went weak, her heart thundering in her ears as she suddenly realized what Zach was doing. It was why they had all gathered here, why Zach wouldn't let her drink too much. Tradition.

He handed off his champagne glass to Hailey, went down on one knee, and held up a diamond solitaire ring. "Carrie, will you do me the honor of becoming my wife?"

"Yes!" she cried, rushing to him.

He slid the ring on her finger and rose to his feet, pulling her into his arms. Their friends and family gathered close, congratulating them, and it was exactly as Zach had described. The culmination and full meaning of the courtship ritual. A long tradition continuing on with them. Extraordinary because neither of them had been looking for forever. Hadn't believed it was possible. But it was wonderfully possible because they were meant to be.

A short while later, the photographer and reporter approached. "We'd love to feature your wedding in the magazine," the woman said. "From engagement to wedding preparations to the wedding."

Carrie turned to Hailey. "Did you plan all this?"

Hailey lifted her palms. "I planned the proposal with Zach, not the magazine's interest in your wedding."

The reporter added, "Of course, the magazine will pick up the expense of a first-class wedding."

Carrie exchanged a look with Zach. "We'd love to!"

"And now we celebrate," Zach said. "Have as much champagne as you want." He handed her a glass.

She took a long swallow. "Really? As much as I want?"

"No," Zach and her friends said in near unison.

"Carrie, you get crazy after two glasses," Hailey said. "Last time you ended up picking up a stranger and getting engaged to the guy." She looked thoughtful. "Hmm, maybe not such a bad plan. Maybe it would work again for another couple."

And then music started playing, a romantic slow song. Hailey snatched the glass from Carrie's hand.

Zach pulled Carrie into his arms. "Dancing is important to the courtship ritual."

"Dr. Harrison, you're making me so hot." She threw her arms around his neck and peppered him with kisses.

He kissed her back. And then they danced, their friends and family gradually filling in around them.

Zach leaned down, whispering in her ear, "How many children, Carrie?"

She smiled, glad he knew her well enough to know she wanted them. And also glad that he did too. "Two would be nice."

He stopped dancing and framed her face with his hands. "Agreed." His voice dropped low and deep. "Do you have any idea how much I love you?"

"Yes," she whispered. "Because that's how much I love you."

He brushed his lips over hers. "You need a reminder."

"I do," she breathed. "Have your wicked way with me."

He kissed her. "I will soon. Count on it."

They beamed at each other.

After the dance, which it seemed everyone had taken pictures of, including the *Bride Special* photographer, Zach insisted they thank each person individually for sharing in their celebration.

Finally, they went back home and consummated the union.

The vows would have to wait.

But in their hearts, they'd already happened.

Dear Readers,

Did Josh and Hailey turn the corner in their frenemy war? After all, he helped her out with that *Bride Special* interview. Though there is still the matter of five hundred large standing between them. LOL Ethan Case might've been distracted with all of Hailey's unusual flirting, but now his eyes are open to the challenge of a woman who firmly believes a vibrator is better than a man. Next up is Ethan and Ally's story, *Mess With Me*, book 6 in the Happy Endings Book Club series. Join the club and get your happy ending!

Mess With Me

Ally Bloom attends her college reunion on a mission—a second chance with her first love. Turns out he's single and… not interested. Their love is doomed! But when Ethan Case, the sexy cop friend of a friend, finds her crying in her spiked punch, he invites her for coffee with his date. Knowing he's taken and she doesn't need to impress him, Ally blurts the entire sucky men saga that is her love life.

But wait! There he is at her Happy Endings Book Club meeting.

And pulling her over for speeding.

And in her classroom to talk to the kids about safety.

Is the man just messing with her or is this the beginning of something real?

Sign up for my newsletter and never miss a new release! kyliegilmore.com/newsletter

ALSO BY KYLIE GILMORE

Unleashed Romance <<steamy romcoms with dogs!

Fetching (Book 1)

Dashing (Book 2)

Sporting (Book 3)

Toying (Book 4)

Blazing (Book 5)

Chasing (Book 6)

Daring (Book 7)

Leading (Book 8)

Racing (Book 9)

Loving (Book 10)

The Clover Park Series <<brothers who put family first!

The Opposite of Wild (Book 1)

Daisy Does It All (Book 2)

Bad Taste in Men (Book 3)

Kissing Santa (Book 4)

Restless Harmony (Book 5)

Not My Romeo (Book 6)

Rev Me Up (Book 7)

An Ambitious Engagement (Book 8)

Clutch Player (Book 9)

A Tempting Friendship (Book 10)

Clover Park Bride: Nico and Lily's Wedding

A Valentine's Day Gift (Book 11)

Maggie Meets Her Match (Book 12)

The Clover Park STUDS series <<hawt geeks who unleash into studs!

Almost Over It (Book 1)

Almost Married (Book 2)

Almost Fate (Book 3)

Almost in Love (Book 4)

Almost Romance (Book 5)

Almost Hitched (Book 6)

Happy Endings Book Club Series <<the Campbell family and a romance book club collide!

Hidden Hollywood (Book 1)

Inviting Trouble (Book 2)

So Revealing (Book 3)

Formal Arrangement (Book 4)

Bad Boy Done Wrong (Book 5)

Mess With Me (Book 6)

Resisting Fate (Book 7)

Chance of Romance (Book 8)

Wicked Flirt (Book 9)

An Inconvenient Plan (Book 10)

A Happy Endings Wedding (Book 11)

The Rourkes Series <<swoonworthy princes and kickass princesses!

Royal Catch (Book 1)

Royal Hottie (Book 2)

Royal Darling (Book 3)

Royal Charmer (Book 4)

Royal Player (Book 5)

Royal Shark (Book 6)

Rogue Prince (Book 7)

Rogue Gentleman (Book 8)

Rogue Rascal (Book 9)

Rogue Angel (Book 10)

Rogue Devil (Book 11)

Rogue Beast (Book 12)

Check out my website for the most up-to-date list of my books:
kyliegilmore.com/books

ABOUT THE AUTHOR

Kylie Gilmore is the *USA Today* bestselling author of the Unleashed Romance series, the Rourkes series, the Happy Endings Book Club series, the Clover Park series, and the Clover Park STUDS series. She writes humorous romance that makes you laugh, cry, and reach for a cold glass of water.

Kylie lives in New York with her family, two cats, and a nutso dog. When she's not writing, reading hot romance, or dutifully taking notes at writing conferences, you can find her flexing her muscles all the way to the high cabinet for her secret chocolate stash.

Sign up for Kylie's Newsletter and get a FREE book! kyliegilmore.com/newsletter

For text alerts on Kylie's new releases, text KYLIE to the number (888) 707-3025. (US only)

For more fun stuff check out Kylie's website https://www.kyliegilmore.com.

Thanks for reading *Bad Boy Done Wrong*. I hope you enjoyed it. Would you like to know about new releases? You can sign up for my new release email list at kyliegilmore.com/newsletter. I promise not to clog your inbox! Only new release info, sales, and some fun giveaways.

I love to hear from readers! You can find me at:
    kyliegilmore.com
    Instagram.com/kyliegilmore
    Facebook.com/KylieGilmoreToo
    Twitter @KylieGilmoreToo

If you liked Zach and Carrie's story, please leave a review on your favorite retailer's website or Goodreads. Thank you.